AMY TASUKADA

THE DEAFENING SILENCE

The Yakuza Path: The Deafening Silence:
© 2018 Amy Tasukada

ISBN Paper: 978-1-948361-09-5

Cover Design: Natasha Snow

Book Interior Design: Ampersand Book Interiors

ACKNOWLEDGEMENTS

Thank you to my husband and family, without whose love and support this book would probably not be here. Lorelai, who was a constant cheerleader even when I complained to her about various bookish things. The other awesome people who read the book at various drafts, Nell Iris, Addison Albright, and Michelle. Jhericca and Elise for their friendship and picking out some awesome names.

Finally, you. Thank you for giving my book a try.

CHAPTER 1

AKI HAD EVERY step of the theft planned.

He and Nao would check into their hotel rooms. Aki had doubled-checked they'd be beside each other before their flight to Hokkaido left. Then they'd head off to Odori Park to view the snow sculptures. They were no match for the floats of the Gion festival back home in Kyoto, but Nao would still enjoy the culture surrounding the crafted pieces. If Aki was lucky, he'd get Nao to smile when he pointed out the white flurries in Nao's hair from the fluttering snow.

Dinner would be at a family-owned soup curry restaurant. Sapporo was the birthplace of the meal, and Aki would effortlessly answer all the questions Nao asked about the unique dish. Once the food arrived, Nao would relax and tell a few childhood stories like he always did during their shared meals. If the need struck him, Aki would tell his own. They'd be so lost in conversation they wouldn't notice the restaurant closing

around them. Once they realized, they'd apologize and head back to the hotel.

Nao would be so impressed with Aki's meticulously planned evening, he'd stop Aki before they parted to their sperate rooms. Nao's deep voice asking if Aki would like to have a drink in his would make Aki shudder. The light fluttering in Aki's chest would grow until it pounded his chest like an odaiko drum at a festival.

He'd enter Nao's room, unsure of where to sit at first, but then Nao would motion to the bed. Aki wouldn't be able to stop his grin, because at that moment he'd know his plan had worked. The trip to Sapporo lured Nao's heart away from his beloved Kyoto. With his boss finally out of his city, Aki would finally steal his heart.

Nao would offer him a drink, and Aki would accept. Aki would drink it too quickly and get hit with the intoxicating buzz that would make his skin flush. Nao would join him on the bed and put his empty glass on the nightstand.

He'd lean a little closer.

His hot breath would caress Aki's neck.

Aki would try to swallow back the desire building within him, but the glint in Nao's eyes would only encourage his growing erection. It would take all of Aki's strength not to fall to his knees right there.

Then Nao would open his mouth and say what Aki had been waiting for since the accidental kiss they'd shared. Aki could die he'd be so happy.

Nao would lean closer.

Their hands would brush, and for once Nao would allow his fingers to linger there. Aki's skin would tinkle with each stroke of Nao's fingers along his open palm. So gentle yet deliberate. Aki would swallow and fight the image of Nao stroking other parts of his body with the same vigor.

Aki, Nao would say to him. There's something I must confess—

Kohta's screeching laugh sliced through Aki's fantasy worse than a papercut underneath his nail.

Aki groaned and turned the printed hotel confirmation paper over, reminding himself he'd reserved four rooms not two. The trip to Japan's northernmost island wasn't some weekend getaway but a business trip to solidify the alliance between the Kyoto Matsukawa and the Sapporo Mafufugumi. The Sapporo godfather probably had his own ideas of how to show Nao a good time, which meant all of Aki's carefully chosen excursions lived on as nothing more than figments in Aki's lascivious daydream.

When they'd arrived at the hotel, Nao had followed Kohta and Jun to the bar, leaving Aki in charge of dealing with the rooms. Kohta and Jun had gotten their drinks, and together they'd all moved to one of the lush seating areas in the lobby, where Kohta's laughter was getting side-eyed by everyone who passed.

Aki crossed his arms and shifted his weight to his other foot. "Next, please," the concierge said.

His red jacket had the hotel's brand over the handkerchief pocket. He smiled as Aki approached.

"I have a reservation under Hisona." Aki presented the paper bill.

"Aki Hisona?"

"Correct."

The concierge nodded. "One moment, please."

Another one of Kohta's laughs bubbled up through the soft murmurs of the other guests in the lounge. Aki sighed. When Kohta and Jun got together, there was no stopping the lurid tales of their sexual escapades. Each one tried to top the other with their jokes and bragging stories. Aki glared at Kohta, but, of course, the fake blond was completely oblivious to how annoying he was. Aki's jaw clenched.

He hated Nao's decision to promote Kohta to his bodyguard after only a few months of training. Aki hated how the peaceful alone time he'd share with Nao every morning had been turned into a loud party of three, but what Aki hated the most was how Kohta's wavy blond locks resembled Nao's dead lover. Aki had lost count of the times he'd seen a flutter of attraction in Nao's eyes only for it to turn into forlorn longing with one glance at Kohta. The resemblance made it impossible to compete with him for their boss's affection, even if Kohta was only interested in fondling half-drunk women.

"Are the rooms ready?" Aki asked.

"Sorry about the delay, Mr. Hisona. It will be another minute."

The concierge picked up the phone then whispered something. With Jun and Kohta's blabbering, Aki couldn't make out what was said.

The lobby door opened to let in an older couple. Their slow

pace allowed more of the February chill to spill over the check-in desk. Aki tugged at his coat collar. Checking into hotel rooms never took this long.

The concierge had stepped away and was replaced with someone wearing a pin that read "Head Manager."

"Excuse me, Mr. Hisona?"

"Is there a problem?" Aki tapped his fingers on the counter.

The manager pointed toward Nao and the others. "Are those gentlemen members of your party?"

Aki narrowed his eyes. "I spoke with Sakura earlier today, and she confirmed my reservation."

"So, those gentlemen are with you."

"I would like my rooms."

"I'm sorry, sir, but we don't serve your kind here."

Aki's mouth dropped. Sure, he was a quarter Korean but that hadn't stopped anyone before.

"Excuse me?" Aki said.

"The anti-yakuza laws make it very clear. We—"

"You're not doing business with them. The reservation is under my name, Hisona. Look me up. I have no criminal record. So you can accept my money."

Aki had even taken the extra precaution of flipping over his lapel pin so as to not show the inward-facing arrows of the Matsukawa mob crest. To any outsider, he had no affiliation with the yakuza.

"I'm sorry, Mr. Hisona. The law is very clear that any association will not be tolerated."

Aki ran his fingers through his hair and tried to take in a

deep breath. "I made the reservation weeks ago, and you were happy to accept my money then."

"If we do business with you, all the hotel's bank accounts could become frozen. We cannot take such a risk."

"We have the legitimate right to assembly. You are violating—"

"You and your party need to leave the premises immediately, or I will have to call the police."

Aki pressed his lips into a thin line.

The last thing they needed was for the police to get involved. They weren't back at home, and there was no telling how the police chief would react to a foreign mob coming into the city. Worst case, he'd snatch Nao on some minor crime and hold a press conference about bringing down the Kyoto kingpin.

Aki grabbed the printed reservation and folded it back into his coat pocket. "Fine."

Aki fought the urge to scream. Getting everyone checked into the hotel was Aki's first duty outside of Kyoto, and he'd failed Nao. Aki's stomach churned with each step toward Nao and the others.

Four identical white leather chairs faced each other, flanked by a glass surround fire place. Jun and Kohta sat beside each other, leaving the chair directly beside Nao empty.

Kohta brushed back his hair over his shoulder, showing more of the striped neon green and pink shirt. Fortunately for everyone's eyesight, he masked most of the garish design under a black blazer.

Jun kept to the standard yakuza uniform of a suit and tie

even if he looked like he was playing dress-up. Though he was in his late thirties, he kept the baby face of a boy entering high school. He'd probably been carded when he'd ordered the drink he sipped on between tales.

"You should see the girls the Mafufugumi have," Jun said. "Like nothing you've seen before. Their liaison Shinji knows all the best ones. So make sure to get on his good side for the prime choice."

"Really? What makes them so special?"

"They're all foreign, so even if they talk back, you don't have to listen."

Kohta laughed, slamming his fist on the chair's leather arm as Jun snickered into his whiskey glass.

Nao ignored them, instead gazing into the light of the fireplace beside the group. The glass front reflected his handsome face, and his long black hair kissed his neck. His cold stare was intimidating on the best days. His lean muscles hid underneath his Japanese-made tailored suit, but Aki knew with a single punch, Nao could break bones.

Aki rubbed his palms on his pants, knowing how quickly Nao could turn when things didn't go his way.

"I humbly apologize for disturbing you, Father Murata," Aki managed to squeak out, thickening his Kyoto accent and using all the formality their godfather deserved. Calling Nao Murata only by his first name was an intimacy Aki could only reserve for his innermost thoughts.

"Is it me, or are the women hotter in Hokkaido?" Kohta elbowed Jun and pointed. "Like damn."

Nao hadn't even turned toward Aki.

Aki started again, a little louder. "I humbly—"

"Will you two shut your mouths already," Nao hissed.

He glared at them. Kohta and Jun immediately stopped their chatter, but Nao kept his glare locked on them. Nao could pick apart someone like a buzzard feeding on the bones of roadkill. The air grew heavy around them, and they remained silent enough that even the ice settling in Jun's drink rang out like a gunshot.

"Forgive me, Father Murata, I got carried away," Jun said.

"Don't do it to me. You both need to apologize to Aki."

Aki's cheeks grew hot. He didn't need an apology from such a high-ranking family member.

Jun cleared his throat and leaned back in his chair. "I was rude, Hisona. Let me buy you a drink as an apology."

Kohta echoed his apology, and Aki nodded and accepted both of their offers. Then Nao's sharp brown eyes turned to meet Aki's, and all the muscles in his body tensed.

"Are the rooms ready?" Nao asked.

Aki couldn't even do that right. He didn't deserve the patience and respect Nao had shown him. The muscles in his jaw quivered.

Nao narrowed his eyes. "What happened?"

"They won't allow me to check in."

"That's impossible," Jun said. "The Mafufugumi suggested this hotel."

"They quoted the anti-yakuza law and said we needed to leave," Aki said.

Jun jerked his head to Aki. "You must've fucked up."

"When I made the reservation, everything was fine."

"Who waited on you? You must've talked to the wrong person and tipped them off or something."

Aki bit his tongue.

He wasn't incompetent. He'd reviewed the list of hotels Jun had suggested and found the one that suited Nao's tastes best. Jun had never mentioned needing to talk with a specific person.

Still, Aki couldn't defend himself. Jun led the street side of the Matsukawa, meaning he worked directly under Nao. Jun had more status in the family even if Aki had a more intimate relationship with their leader. As Nao's secretary, Aki's biggest responsibility was picking what tea to serve each morning and answering his phone.

"Forgive me for my ignorance," Aki said. "Perhaps another..."

Aki trailed off as two security guards rounded the corner. One had a thin mustache, while the other talked into a radio. They stopped behind Jun and Kohta.

"You need to leave," the mustached guard said.

Nao opened his arms. "Your hotel needs to reconsider their previous statement. We're willing to be paying guests."

"Hey now, take it easy there."

Kohta rolled his eyes. "We're not the ones making this difficult."

Radio Guard finished calling for backup and put a hand on his baton. "It's time to move along now. If you know what's good for you."

Nao stood and pulled on his coat. "There's no need to make

threats. We'll get on our way as soon as my friends here pay for their drinks."

Aki bit the inside of his cheek. Perhaps the Mafufugumi didn't wield as much strength as the Matsukawa did back home. Though it could simply be a matter of not investing enough in tourism to make a trusting relationship with hotels like Nao did back home. One thing was for sure: whatever connection the Mafufugumi had with the hotel had vanished.

Jun spat. "You guys can suck—"

The glare Nao shot Jun stopped him mid-insult. "We don't want to cause a scene."

"I apologize." Jun bowed.

"Good. Now pay and then leave," Nao said between clenched teeth. "I don't want any of us landing on the front page because you forgot to pay a bar tab."

"You need to listen to your friend there and go," the guard said.

The guard jerked Jun's arm to pull him up. Jun threw his other arm back, fingers balled into a fist. The guard whipped out his baton and threw Jun to the ground. The guard jumped on him, twisting Jun's arm behind his back.

"What the fuck? Get off me!" Jun struggled to break free.

"Stop resisting," the guard yelled and delivered a hard blow with his baton to the side of Jun's face.

The other guard joined in the beating.

Aki flinched with each blow to Jun. After the third slam to Jun's face, Aki had to look away. Each swing bit into Aki like a punch in the gut for his failure. His fingers found their way into his pockets, and he balled up the hotel reservation. He crumbled it up. Not an hour into Sapporo and he'd brought shame to the whole family.

Kohta took his position between Nao and the hotel's security, finally acting like the bodyguard he was.

"We should probably go," Kohta mumbled.

With Kohta escorting Nao outside, it left Aki to grab everyone's luggage. He grabbed the handle of Nao's bag, and Jun let out a defeated moan. Blood covered his face and dropped onto the carpet.

"Go on! Git!" the guard yelled at Aki as a group of hotel staff tried to keep everyone back, but it was impossible. A small crowd had formed, and everyone had their phones out, flashing photos or recording the video.

Aki snatched the rest of the luggage and scurried outside. The last thing he needed was to be on some news report associated with the yakuza, putting his key position as the clean secretary in danger. In the end, it probably didn't matter. The whole fiasco fell on his shoulders, and he'd have to endure Nao's punishment.

CHAPTER 2

$\cdot \cdot \cdot$

CAUSING EVEN THE smallest scene was dangerous, and Nao Murata had expected Jun to be able to control his volatile temper. Nao's gaze stayed locked on Jun even as Kohta shuffled him out of the hotel. They weren't back home, and the last thing the Matsukawa needed was for news to pick up on Nao's absence from Kyoto.

The sightings of the Korean mob in Matsukawa territory were becoming an almost-daily occurrence. There had been enough tension between the family and the Korean mob when Nao was home, but if the Koreans realized the Matsukawa were without him, they'd take the opportunity to strike.

Once they were outside, Kohta whistled. "They're really fucking him over."

"Authorities always get a hard-on beating the shit out of yakuza," Nao said. "They know we won't complain about mistreatment."

When he'd served out his juvenile sentence, he'd seen plenty

of guards with tents in their pants when punishing him for the smallest indiscretion. They'd happily gloat about whipping the son of the local mob into obedience.

"He'll be lucky if he has any teeth left," Kohta said.

"They were strangely quick to act. It seems odd."

People strolled through the automatic doors, unaware of the scene inside. Nao walked farther away from the entry since the tall evergreens blocked the view of the road. When the cops came, Nao wanted to make sure they weren't accompanied by any press.

"Where's Aki?" Nao asked.

"He was right behind us."

"Well, he's not anymore. Go find him. Make sure the security hasn't gotten him involved in Jun's mess."

Kohta took a few steps toward the entry, but then Aki scurried out of the hotel doors. The luggage wheels scraped over the pebbled pass-through of the valet parking as he positioned himself beside Nao. Nao grinned. Aki had even managed to snag Kohta's monstrosity of a red suitcase with *LV* in the center. It was twice the size necessary for the quick trip.

"I apologize for all the trouble my lack of judgment has caused." Aki fell to the ground, bowing so low his head touched the pebbled walkway. "It was irresponsible, and I know I should not be forgiven…"

Aki's apology continued. With each new phrase, his Kyoto dialect thickened and came out so luscious Nao couldn't help but close his eyes and taste each syllable. It was almost as delicious as his favorite oolong tea. When the sirens of cop cars opened

Nao's eyes, he caught Aki's trembling left hand, but Nao knew better than to keep Aki in his agony.

"Get up. We shouldn't have trouble finding another hotel." Nao gave a half smile. "Kohta and I will wait in the taxi next time."

Aki brushed off his pants and stood. "Of course, I'll get on it right away. I won't fail you again."

He poked around on his phone as four cops got out of the cars and marched into the hotel. Nao turned up the collar of his long black coat.

Kohta shook his head. "Jun's screwed if they brought that many."

Jun would be fine.

It was Nao who was screwed.

Jun had been the sole liaison of the soon-to-be alliance between the Matsukawa and the Mafufugumi. Like in all alliances between families, no godfather would talk directly until the day of the sake ceremony. Nao didn't even know what the Sapporo godfather looked like, and with only six months of being the active godfather to Nao's name, the finer nuances of forming a new alliance eluded him.

Nao clenched his fists.

"At least they didn't grab you, eh?" Kohta said.

Kohta could be as dimwitted as his clothing choices were loud, but his accuracy with a gun could rival Nao's.

A limo pulled through the hotel's valet and stopped a safe distance from the entry where Nao and the others had gathered. The driver stepped out and opened the door for his occupant, whose swagger could be nothing more than a fellow yakuza godfather. Nao pulled his shoulders back and stood straight.

Watanabe, the godfather of the Mafufugumi, stood in front of Nao, not hiding the fact he was sizing up his younger counterpart. Watanabe's black fur coat added another twenty pounds to his girth. Gray speckled Watanabe's hair, and his bushy eyebrows looked like silkworms on his face. He might've been taller, but Nao was in better shape.

"Mr. Murata, nice to meet you." Watanabe stuck out his hand.

Nao took it in a firm handshake with a bow. "It's a pleasure to finally meet you."

"Where is Jun? He was supposed to help with all this."

"He's—"

"Fuck you all!" Jun yelled.

The hotel doors opened, and four cops stormed out, holding on to each of Jun's limbs. Blood trickled from his nose and dribbled down his chin before splattering onto the brown-pebbled entry. The police threw Jun into the back of a patrol car.

Kurosawa had suggested Jun to be the street leader, and Nao had vaguely remembered his name being said when Nao was a teen. Jun's brashness was good for dealing with the dirtier side of the Matsukawa, and once war broke out again with the Korean mob, he'd be a valuable leader. Though anytime he had to deal with an authority, he failed at tact and became reduced to a swearing good-for-nothing.

"That's some bad luck." Watanabe laughed, his eyes eaten by his caterpillar-like eyebrows.

Nao puffed out his chest, but his stomach twisted like a rolled oolong tea leaf.

With Jun in custody, it weakened the Matsukawa's already broken hand in the budding alliance between the two families. The Mafufugumi had the relationship with the police. They'd be the ones to set Jun free, adding yet another favor they'd be performing. As formal allies, Nao wouldn't be able to control when the favors would be called in. It was exactly what the Matsukawa didn't need.

"Stuff like this happens," Watanabe said. "Why don't you come with me so we're not caught up in this mess?"

"Of course." Nao readjusted his tie.

Watanabe was too casual about the whole situation. Either he was trying to save Nao's face, or he was up to something more suspicious. Nao couldn't shake the nagging feeling that Watanabe had pulled up at exactly the worst time.

They climbed into the limo. Four other Mafufugumi members were inside, which meant more of their family witnessed how incompetent the Matsukawa looked, putting Nao in the running for the worst godfather in all of Japan.

"Don't worry," Watanabe said as one of his lackeys poured everyone champagne. "The hotels are meticulous about anti-yakuza laws during tourist season."

Nao tapped his finger against the bottom of the champagne flute. "I see."

Aki wouldn't make a reservation at a hotel without checking how comfortable they were with yakuza guests. Aki wasn't an idiot; he always knew exactly what Nao needed before he even opened his mouth.

"Since hotels are hard to come by, your men can stay at our headquarters, and it would be my pleasure to have you stay at my family house. I won't have to worry about you making googly eyes at my wife." Watanabe winked.

Nao was already separated from the man who knew Watanabe best, and Watanabe's offer would sever Nao's proximity from the remaining two. Nao had already abandoned Jun. Nao squeezed the flute a little tighter. What would Aki and Kohta think if he cut them loose too?

Kohta downed his glass of champagne, and a Mafufugumi poured him another. He'd be fine by himself, but Aki? He still hadn't looked up from his shoes the whole ride.

Nao shifted in his seat, pressing a foot alongside Aki's. A small smile crossed Aki's heart-shaped face, and his large brown eyes shone. He wouldn't last long without him. No one would dare spout an offhanded comment about Nao's homosexuality to his face, but if Aki was staying the night with the Mafufugumi…

Nao slipped his foot away and glanced toward the tinted windows. The alliance would be formalized at dinner, so no one would dare lay a hand on Aki after that. Still, Nao would tell Kohta to keep an eye on him. It was best to get on Watanabe's good side to build the mobs' lasting alliance. One night wouldn't hurt.

"Thank you for the generous offer. We accept." Nao held up his glass.

"I'll make sure one of our cops handles Jun's case."

"He will be happy knowing that."

"We have to protect our own."

Nao smiled. "Exactly."

Kohta downed two more flutes of champagne and complimented the fine Sapporo women. He would be worthless if he was drunk off his ass, but before he'd joined the underworld, he'd been a host. Nao knew Kohta could hold his alcohol and function fine. His choice of conversation was a different story altogether, but it made Watanabe laugh, so Kohta's charms apparently worked.

"I once went to Kyoto," Watanabe said. "It's a very beautiful city. I really enjoyed those geisha."

"Kyoto *geiko* are world famous," Nao corrected Watanabe.

One of his eyebrows lowered, but he held up his glass again. "Then to the geiko of Kyoto."

They all clinked their glasses together and called cheers. All the while, Nao could feel the tug of Kyoto on his heart. The looming threat of the Koreans trying to carve up the city still pressed heavy on him. At any moment, Aki's phone could ring, bringing news of a Korean attack.

It didn't take long for the limo to pull up at a restaurant called Molière. With a name like that, would they even have sake to perform the ceremony?

"This is the best restaurant in all of Sapporo," Watanabe said.

"How interesting."

Watanabe chuckled. "You have French restaurants in Kyoto, don't you?"

"I wouldn't know."

"Jun warned me that you were into traditional things. You'll be in for a treat."

Inside, plush carpet greeted Nao, along with a menu more French than Japanese. They were taken to a bathroom away from the other guests, but with the most garish silvery pink wallpaper that was so garish even Kohta would pass on it even if it was from his favorite designer.

Watanabe ordered two of everything off the menu. Nao randomly pointed at something for his meal and felt dirty for even doing that much.

"Your flight wasn't bad?" Watanabe asked.

"Long."

"Jun told me you don't leave Kyoto."

Nao ran his finger along the cloth napkin in his lap. Maybe he should've talked to Jun about not giving away his whole life history to someone who still wasn't an ally. All Jun had told him about Watanabe was that he liked the deal and had a booming porn and prostitution business.

"What about you?" Watanabe arched his eyebrow at Aki. "What do you think of Sapporo?"

"It's colder than I imagined."

"It's a dry cold, and you came during our blizzard season."

"So I should've brought a different coat."

Watanabe laughed, but Aki's words stabbed Nao. He wasn't speaking in the long elegant Kyoto dialect like he did back home, but shorter and standardized sentences like a Tokyo office worker. It was like giving a renowned calligraphy artist a cheap pen instead of a brush to do his work.

Nao's nostrils flared. "Why are you speaking like that?"

Aki bit his lip. "I humbly beg forgiveness. I only want to make sure everyone could understand."

"You're from Kyoto. I'm from Kyoto. Even fucking Kohta's

from Kyoto. These guys know where we come from. Are you not proud you're from Kyoto?"

"I am proud."

"When you change your accent, you sound like an ungrateful bastard."

"Excuse me, I…" Aki opened his mouth, but nothing further came out.

Aki's Adam's apple bobbed as he swallowed. The sheen to his brown eyes made them appear even larger, and once his speech was correct, Aki would turn into the handsome man Nao knew.

"I humbly plead for your forgiveness, which I do not deserve," Aki said. "It was a mistake I swear on all the stars in the sky will never happen again."

"Good."

A wide grin struck Watanabe's face. At least he seemed amused so far. All Nao wanted was to get the ceremony over with and sleep until his flight tomorrow afternoon. No part of Japan could live up to Kyoto's care for tradition. It was Kyoto that kept Japanese culture alive despite people like Watanabe throwing his money at a foreign place.

If the alliance wasn't out of necessity, Nao would have never left the city.

Kyoto needed him.

The food came out, cutting short Watanabe's story of how he busted the knee caps of someone who was two weeks late on their debt payment.

Each dish looked inedible, and Nao couldn't even recognize half of the food. He grabbed his knife and cut through his cod.

He ate a few bites. It was all right, but his fish could've drowned in all the cream sauce. Even ramen from a vending machine would've tasted better.

A waiter refilled everyone's wineglasses, but when he came around to Nao, he covered it with his hand.

"Sake," Nao said.

"Sake, sir?"

"Did the Japanese confuse you? I want sake, now."

The hair on the waiter's hand stood on end. "Right away, sir."

"We're starting this already?" Watanabe asked.

"Dinner seems like the best time."

"You youngsters can be so eager."

"Some would say that's what makes the Matsukawa so efficient."

Nao leaned back in his chair. At twenty-six, it put at least thirty years between him and Watanabe. Nao might've been the youngest godfather in Japan, but he knew better than to let the fact make him a doormat.

"I was going to wait until we met up with Shinji and showed you the real entertainment the Mafufugumi could offer," Watanabe said.

"Well, I hate to waste good sake."

The waiter brought the sake and set it along with two bowl-like cups in front of Nao.

Nao poured some sake into his bowl, and Watanabe did the same to his.

"To the union of the Matsukawa and the Mafufugumi," Nao said and took his sip from his cup.

Watanabe raised his cup but didn't take a sip. "How many Koreans did you kill that night? They said you killed over a hundred with only a sword."

"That night, I single-handedly saved Kyoto from the Korean mob trying to carve it up. No other city with Korean scum taking root there has been able to do it."

"Are you a demon now?"

Some of the Mafufugumi failed at holding back their laughter. Nao's eyes narrowed, and he leaned forward.

"What exactly do you mean by that?"

"You haven't heard the Hokkaido saying? If you kill a hundred people, it turns you into a demon. You killed all those Koreans, so you must be a demon now." Watanabe set his sake bowl back on the table. "I'm not sure if I'm ready to make a deal with a devil yet."

CHAPTER 3

· · ·

NAO'S FINGERS CURLED around his sake bowl until he clutched it in his fist. It would be so easy to slam it against Watanabe's squirmy eyebrows. The gash in his head would make his smirk disappear. His dripping blood would match all those sauces he'd slurped up during dinner.

"Double-crossing a devil doesn't sound very smart," Nao said between clenched teeth.

"Double-crossing?" Watanabe laughed. "This is a renegotiation of terms."

"Slaughtering the Koreans wasn't some far-gone memory from youth. It happened months ago. You knew who you were dealing with when you were discussing it with Jun."

"It's different meeting you in person." Watanabe motioned toward Nao's death grip on the sake bowl. "I see how blood-thirsty you are."

Nao didn't ease his grip off the bowl. Rejecting an already

established agreement was wrong, and without Jun here, Watanabe probably had zero guilt about it. Worse, Nao had been rejected, not only in front of his own men but the Mafufugumi's as well. They'd immediately see how unbalanced the alliance was, and Watanabe's men would never see the Matsukawa as equals.

Nao pushed his sake bowl on the table and leaned back in his chair. "You old bosses like to string out these simple meetings into long affairs."

"You're taking this to mean something else." Watanabe leaned forward. "Hear me out."

"It wouldn't be smart to reject the deal we already agreed upon."

"I want to make sure we have the resources needed to fulfill our need for the agreement. A little sweetening of the offer is all I'm asking. You do want us to maintain contact with the real godmother of the Matsukawa."

A fiery heat rushed through Nao's body. Watanabe dared undermined his authority as leader. Each of Nao's muscles quivered with the desire to attack. Nao could've shoved his sake bowl down Watanabe's throat right there before his men even realized what was going on. Nao's butter knife could stab the eye of the Mafufugumi to Watanabe's right. While the left one was too shocked to act, Nao could secure him in a headlock and slowly watch the veins pop out of his neck as he suffocated.

Last year, the Korean mafia had slaughtered Nao's father. They had gone so far as to pluck his eyeballs out of his skull and deliver them to Matsukawa headquarters in a champagne glass. He'd named Miko as his successor, but the month before, she'd been sent to a Sapporo prison. She'd appointed Nao as active godfather while she served her sentence, but all major decisions needed to be filtered through her.

All the Mafufugumi had to do was maintain their contact in the prison and deliver messages back and forth between the Matsukawa and Miko.

Nao bit his tongue. The copper taste of blood took the edge off enough for him to think. He couldn't attack another yakuza family unprovoked without starting a war. The Matsukawa couldn't leave without the alliance. Maybe if he played dumb, Watanabe would realize how stupid double-crossing a soon-to-be ally was.

"You're in luck," Nao said. "Kyoto has the best confectionary shops in all of Japan. I can have my men ship a variety up, and as long as the weather holds, you'll have them by morning."

"You're funny." Watanabe laughed and elbowed the man next to him. "Did Jun tell you he was funny?"

The man shook his head.

"He must've told Shinji then about Murata's sense of humor."

All doubt in Nao's mind that Watanabe had tipped off the hotel grew more and more. He'd pulled up at exactly the worst moment. It was too much of a coincidence if it hadn't been planned. Without Jun as mediator, Watanabe could ask for whatever he wanted, and Nao would be at his mercy because Nao couldn't say no.

"Yatsuhashi cookies are particularly delicious," Nao continued. "But I know a place that still makes mochi the traditional way. I can make sure we send you a sweet collection fit for the emperor each month."

"See? Hilarious. Maybe you should be a comedian."

"What kinds of sweets do you want boxed up?"

"Women."

Nao grinned, patted Kohta's shoulder. "It's a good thing I brought Kohta along, then, isn't it? He knows all about women. They're not to my particular taste."

Kohta beamed. "Don't worry. I'll make sure we send up some of the best Kyoto prostitutes."

"I already have a supply established with the Russian mob," Watanabe said. "I don't need that from your family."

"Don't you find dealing with a foreign mob disgusting?" Nao let out a sharp scoff. "Especially the Russians? They still think Etorofu is theirs. What horrible things have fallen on the Mafufugumi that you have to deal with such a wretched group of people?"

Watanabe's eyes narrowed. "Japanese mobs can only provide ladies from the Philippines, but the Russians open the gateway to the West. More exotic women fetch higher prices. It's more profitable. I would like the Matsukawa to handle the next exchange for me. Any devil can agree it's a small price considering you're getting the Mafufugumi's soul."

"I see."

Nao pressed his lips together. No matter how much he hated the idea, he didn't want his first big decision as godfather to screw over the Matsukawa.

"How much is it for these exotic ladies?" Nao asked.

"Only five bars of gold."

Kohta whistled. "Those must be some fine women."

Nao shot him a death glare, and Kohta covered his mouth

with his hand. He mumbled an apology and went back to quietly drinking his champagne. Beside him, Aki folded the edge of the cloth napkin on his lap. Poor guy was probably still nervous as shit with the hotel mix-up. It wasn't his fault Watanabe was being a jerk.

"If you handle it, I'll be happy to drink sake with you," Watanabe said.

Five bars would pay for the necessary upgrade in weapons and manpower when the Korean mob inevitably attacked. They had been a threat since Nao had taken over, and the only way to stop them was full annihilation, but the Matsukawa needed an established secure line of communication with Miko first.

Watanabe pushed aside his sake bowl and took up his wineglass. "I understand. You need to see them in action before making a decision."

"I'm not a bisexual.""

"Don't worry, we got men there, too. The Mafufugumi has something for everyone through our brothel doors," Watanabe said. "Your men are welcomed to sample."

Kohta raised an eyebrow at Nao. Of course he'd be up for it. But getting entangled with a foreign mob was out of the question, even if it was as simple as delivering bars of gold. Russians couldn't be trusted like the Japanese.

"Come on," Watanabe said. "I can show you that these Russian hookers are worth it."

If anything, Nao needed to see if the deal was worth it on their part. Jun had never mentioned the Mafufugumi had teamed with the Russians. If Watanabe had hidden it from

Jun during the preliminary negotiations, then it was probably something Watanabe thought Nao wouldn't like. Watanabe could be hiding more, and during the small delay was Nao's chance to dig it up.

Nao stood. "This is your last chance to impress me."

CHAPTER 4

TWO BOUNCERS FLANKED the doors to a black four-story building, their stance screaming yakuza even without the Mafufugumi crest. A businessman approached one of the bouncers and flashed a black card with a number on it. The bouncer nodded, unhooked the velvet rope, and let him in.

"You'll be in for a treat," Watanabe said.

"How fortunate."

Nao stepped out of the limo, staring at his reflection in the dark glass of the building as the rest of the entourage got out of the limo. Deep within the high-end real state of the city, the brothel appeared to be one of the ultra-exclusive night clubs in the area. So many bosses conducted business in brothels. Nao crossed his arms as snow flurries began to fall around them. Next time he'd pick the brothel, and then he wouldn't have to deal with ladies convincing him he "just hadn't been with the right woman." Maybe it would finally show the other godfathers how boring they were for him.

Kohta's grin couldn't have been any bigger, while Aki kept his hands in his pockets and nervously laughed along to the joke one of the Mafufugumi told. Aki looked too innocent to have even been to a strip club.

Watanabe led the way into the brothel. Everything inside was deep sensuous black or blood-red. Porn played on huge screens mounted on each of the walls. A few women danced on stage, while others were tucked into more private booths. Nao's gaze might've lingered on the details longer, but the only men there were clothed yakuza.

Nao sighed. So much for Watanabe's promise.

Everything appeared new, which impressed Nao even if he hadn't wanted it to. The crowd alone probably provided enough profit to keep a steady cash flow for the Mafufugumi. Still, one of the Matsukawa's values was keeping Japanese traditions alive, and setting up an alliance with a family who had chosen to trade with a foreign power went against it. Thinking about it left a bitter taste in Nao's mouth like an oversteeped tea.

"I think you'll enjoy the more exclusive area," Watanabe said, leaning into Nao to be heard over the thumping music.

Watanabe escorted the group to black doors. He waved to the camera mounted above the doors as they opened. An elevator took them all to the upper level of the brothel. Nao flexed the fingers in his right hand. All of the show had better be worth it.

Aki moved a little closer to Nao. The muscles in Nao's hand loosened, and he put on a faint smile. Aki returned it before his hair covered his face as he looked down. Poor guy was more uncomfortable than the time that body went missing.

"This area we reserve for the highest-level clients," Watanabe said. "Mostly political and a few of the top businessmen from all over the world."

The elevator stopped and let them out into a lush gold interior, soft music creating a comfortable atmosphere. A few lounge areas were scattered in the large room, giving enough privacy between each area. Most of the areas were already occupied with a few women draped in elegant evening dresses.

Watanabe took the group over to a lounge area where a man sat. He was casually dressed and not foreign, so he couldn't be the man Watanabe had decided would change Nao's mind about dealing with foreigners. Still, his sleeveless shirt showed off the guy's toned arms, and his face wasn't bad either.

"This is Shinji," Watanabe said. "He does all the filming for us. All those porn videos playing below were his. He films the women first, and then we bring them here. He also deals with the exchange with the Russians since he can translate."

Shinji's gaze leisurely lingered down Aki's slender body, clearly checking him out and not caring how obvious it was. Who the fuck did Shinji think he was checking out his secretary? Sure, Aki was attractive, and Nao could get lost in his large eyes for hours if he allowed himself, but Aki was working.

"No wonder the videos were so boring," Nao said.

Watanabe laughed. "Well, of course—we all know you enjoy men. Have a seat, order some drinks, and we'll get you set up."

"How generous."

"Really, Murata, this is a time to enjoy yourself. Show your men a good time."

Nao shifted in his seat. His father had made sure to reward his men when they had done a good job. Yakuza work was hard, and even Nao took breaks. Kohta had been begging him to hire another bodyguard for ages since he worked all the time. So maybe it was best to allow him to have a few hours of relief from duty.

A woman poured a drink for all of them, and Nao pretended to enjoy himself and drink half of his glass of champagne. Kohta wrapped an arm around the woman that pored his drink and whispered something in her ear. She laughed, and they chatted some more. All the while, Shinji sat across from Aki and hadn't taken his eyes off him since. Nao couldn't trust the foreign look to Shinji's face or the fact he made it clear Aki was his choice for tonight.

Nao leaned in to Aki and kept his voice low. "Has anyone called?"

Aki pulled out his phone and shook his head. "Still all clear."

"Maybe put it on vibrate since the music is so loud and you're still working."

Nao made sure Shinji heard the last part. Nao kept his eyes locked on the man until Shinji looked away to chat with another Mafufugumi.

After a few minutes, Watanabe send out a stream of Russian women and men.

They all had light-colored hair and eyes, and none of them looked older than twenty-three. Nao shook his head. He was surrounded by men, and the only person he had even an inkling for was Aki. But they could never be together. Nao was married to Kyoto, and the city was a jealous lover. Kyoto would kill Aki if Nao ever dared express his feelings.

"Why don't you and your men try some of our product," Watanabe said. "Maybe after you've had a go, you'll want to do a deal with the Russians to have some shipped to Kyoto."

Kohta grinned and nudged Nao's shoulder. At least with Kohta, everything was predictable.

"Go ahead," Nao sighed.

Kohta went out and grabbed two of the ladies' hands, and Watanabe laughed, too.

If anything, Nao could get some information out of a prostitute. He might know more about the inner workings of Watanabe and his influence. People said things in front of prostitutes, thinking they weren't listening all the time.

Nao grabbed one of the men and tugged him out of the room.

"We'll see if you're right," Nao said.

CHAPTER 5

NAO COULD'VE PLUNGED a knife through Aki's stomach and it would have hurt less.

Aki had convinced himself that Nao was hesitating in moving their relationship forward because he took traditions so seriously. Aki was a quarter Korean, after all, but hoped his unwavering devotion toward Nao would sway Nao's view and could share more than a single heat-of-the-moment kiss again.

All of Aki's fantasies crumbled when Nao casually strolled off with a *Russian* prostitute.

"Anyone caught your eye?" Watanabe asked.

Aki bit his bottom lip to keep it from trembling. He shook his head, too afraid how his voice might sound if he spoke.

An image of the Russian stripping Nao's clothes flashed in Aki's mind. A lump formed in Aki's throat as his stomach folded on itself.

More images flashed.

Nao's eyes becoming clouded by lust.

His hot breath next to the prostitute's ear as he ordered him on the bed.

The whore's head bobbing up and down as he worked on Nao coc—

Aki's stomach burped out rotting decay into his closed mouth, saving him from further thought, but the sickening images had ingrained themselves in his mind.

"Where's the restroom?" Aki asked.

Shinji pointed to the other side of the room. Acid crawled up his throat. He covered his mouth and ran.

The toilets were too far, but he managed to get to the glass-bowl sinks. The buttery sauce from the dinner congealed with half-digested chunks of squid-ink-encrusted cod. The larger pieces slid down the swirling blue sink. The smell alone sent up a second wave of bile, but Aki swallowed it down like his shattered pride. Aki's desperate plan to steal away Nao's heart was worthless. Nao had never wanted a relationship with him in the first place.

"It was stupid to believe," Aki mumbled to himself.

He turned on the faucet and wiped his mouth with the back of his hand.

Of course Nao didn't care about him. Aki was only his secretary. He could barely hold his own when he sparred against the newest recruits in the boxing ring. Aki had read too much into the stolen glances Nao would give him when he thought Aki wasn't looking.

But not some fucking Russian tramp.

The door opened, and Aki looked up to Shinji's reflection in the mirror.

He cocked his head. "You feeling all right?"

"I'm fine." Aki funneled the water from the faucet to clean the edges of the sink.

"You ran off kind of quickly there."

"The flight must've finally gotten to me."

Aki knew better than to insult the restaurant Watanabe took them to, even if he was stringing the Matsukawa along like paper cranes in a chain. The tense atmosphere around Nao hadn't gone unnoticed.

Aki looked away. If only he had his origami paper with him and not in his suitcase. It would give him something to do with his hands and keep his mind off Nao fucking some dirty Russian.

Wait.

Maybe he wasn't fucking him at all. Nao hadn't gone to brothels in months, and the last time he had was to meet Kohta. Kohta had said once Nao realized Kohta was straight, he'd stopped before dicks got taken out. Maybe the same was happening with Nao and the Russian. With the shaky alliance, Nao had to take him to be hospitable toward Watanabe. They might not be fucking at all.

"You guys got cameras in the rooms?" Aki asked, altering his accent and speech to mimic the rest of the Mafufugumi.

Shinji crossed his toned arms and leaned against the wall. "That's kind of kinky, wanting to watch your boss do it."

"That's not what I wanted at all," Aki lied. "Watanabe said politicians and CEOs visit—it would be beneficial to record them in case the Mafufugumi needed blackmail."

"We have cameras, but we don't keep a recording of what

happens in the VIP area. We Mafufugumi take our alliances seriously. We don't have anyone filming your boss and Kohta to use later."

The sink still reeked of vomit, and Aki's throat stung. It would be impossible to know what Nao was doing with the prostitute unless Aki asked, and he was in no position to ask Nao anything.

"We have other guys we can bring out if none of them were to your taste," Shinji said.

"Thank you for your generous offer, but I must humbly decline." Aki let his accent return. What was the point trying to blend in if it didn't get him what he wanted?

Shinji stepped a little close, and Aki looked toward the door. Shinji was an attractive man but hadn't ignited anything within Aki like it did anytime he looked at Nao. When Aki glanced at Nao, he wanted to fold a million cranes in Nao's honor. Aki wanted to improve himself to become worthy of even being by Nao's side. Aki already knew Shinji thought he was attractive by the way he'd checked him out the moment he laid eyes on him. Even if it was clear Shinji was a mix like him. Most yakuza weren't completely Japanese. Still, Aki would be lying if he said he didn't enjoy being looked at that way, but he was working.

"You're not a virgin, are you?" Shinji asked.

"Of course not." Aki scoffed. "I've been with plenty of men."

Shinji grinned, and Aki's cheeks grew hot. He'd never come out to other yakuza, and here Shinji was exposing his inner self like he could read his thoughts. Aki swallowed a deep breath and puffed out his chest. He must've been giving off major *I like cock* vibes for Shinji to figure him out after a few minutes.

Shinji's gazed crawled up and down Aki's body.

Aki rolled his eyes. "Are you seriously doing that again? I just threw up in the sink. How drunk are you to find that attractive?"

Shinji laughed. "I'm not drunk, just intrigued. You're not like the other yakuza I met."

"Did Watanabe send you in here to make sure I was having a good time or something?"

"I wanted to make sure you were okay."

"Well then, thank you for your concern, but I'm perfectly fine."

Shinji grinned. "I can see that. You have to be pretty badass, too, or else you wouldn't be Mr. Murata's secretary."

"No more than any other secretary to a godfather."

"Then there must be a good story behind those."

"Behind what?"

"Those?" Shinji pointed to Aki's discolored hands. "Did acid splash back on you when you were disintegrating Korean mob corpses?"

"More like bad genetics."

Shinji ran his fingers through his hair and shook his head. "I'm really screwing this up, aren't I?"

Aki laughed. "I'm not even sure what you're trying to do."

"Here, will you let me try this again?"

"Try what?"

Shinji's hand glided over Aki's forearm. "Promise me you won't walk out."

"What?"

"Just say you promise."

Aki shook his head. "What are you even doing?"

"Please?"

"Fine."

"Awesome."

Aki had never seen a bigger smile pop on anyone's face. Shinji walked into one of the stalls and closed the door.

"Now forget that we even met," he called.

Aki crossed his arms. The whole act was too strange, a little bit charming in a dorky way, but still odd. Maybe it was a Russian thing.

"Have you forgotten?"

Aki let out a small laugh. At least the odd exchange was better than being in the lounge.

"Okay, I forgot everything," Aki said.

Then he opened the stall door, sweeping back his brown hair, and strolled to the sinks. He paused, allowing his gaze to lap over Aki's body. Occasionally Aki would catch Nao looking at him the same way, but the smile on Shinji's face told Aki something could come of it if he wanted. So often when Nao realized he'd been caught checking Aki out, he'd shake his head, look the other way, and find some silly task to get Aki out of the room.

"Hey." Shinji winked. "I haven't seen you around here before. Nice to meet you. My name's Shinji."

Aki couldn't help but crack a smile. It was too dorky not to.

Shinji gestured to Aki. "And what's your name?"

"Oh." Aki hadn't realized he was supposed to be playing along. He stood up straight, then gave a formal bow. "I'm called Aki Hisona. It's a humbling pleasure to meet you, Shinji. This is my first time in Sapporo, so please look after me."

Shinji smiled. "Don't worry, Aki. I will."

Everything Aki had said spoke with a formality between them, but Shinji called him by his first name, which pushed the conversation into something more intimate. He was attractive, but it was way too soon for that.

"I have a bottle of champagne at my private table. Want to help me finish it off?" Shinji asked. "It might help you get your mind off whatever is bothering you."

Aki moistened his lips. Had he looked that desperate to know what Nao was doing? Kohta had always said he could read Aki's mood like someone playing poker for the first time. Yet the short time he had been with Shinji had been the most enjoyable of the evening.

"A glass sounds nice," Aki said.

He followed Shinji out and away from Mafufugumi at their lounge and to a round booth nestled in a back to corner. Aki couldn't deny that Shinji's tight jeans cupped his ass to make it look extra delectable. Shinji scooted onto a sofa in a corner lounge and a little closer to Aki than necessary.

Someone as attractive as Shinji was probably used to no one speaking up with his instant familiarity. It did feel good to be noticed by someone Aki felt attracted to.

Shinji poured them both a glass and handed one to Aki.

"The music is great here, but it's so hard to hear the person next to you." Shinji leaned into Aki's ear. "Just so you know, I don't care about what's in your pants. It's a person's personality that gets me hot for them."

"How does that fit into the way you look at me? Wouldn't

you have to get to know me first?"

"I couldn't help myself there."

Aki glanced back to the door Nao had walked into. It was taking too long. Wouldn't Nao want to get in and get out? It wasn't like he was on a date.

"If you could do anything, what would it be?" Shinji asked, an irresistible smile plastered on his face.

"What kind of question is that?"

"Is it wrong that I want to get to know you better?"

Aki sighed. "I guess not."

If Nao went along with the alliance, it would be best to have a friendship with some of the Mafufugumi members. Not all yakuza were as friendly toward different sexualities, and with Aki staying at their headquarters, Shinji was probably the best connection he could get.

Shinji stared at him in one of those head-tilted, soon-to-kiss ways.

Aki's cheeks burned, and he looked away.

"Your eyes are amazing," Shinji said.

Aki laughed and took a sip of his champagne. "Yeah? They have bad genetics, too. I have to wear glasses."

"Ahh, that explains why my charms aren't working. They must be blurry."

Shinji had to have been more drunk than he was letting on.

"I wear contacts while I'm working, silly." Aki covered his mouth with his hand.

Shit!

He was drinking too much.

"Oh, well, I'm sure your glasses make you look even cuter."

Nao had said the same thing to Aki once. Aki had started only wearing his glasses then, but then a few weeks later, Nao told him to go back to wearing contacts while he was working.

Aki shook his head and downed the rest of his drink. He held the flute out for Shinji to refill it.

"So," Shinji started, "if you weren't Aki of the Matsukawa, who would you be?"

Aki took another long gulp of his drink, then shrugged. "I used to assemble office furniture, but I wasn't really good at it."

"But what if you could do anything?"

"When I was little, I wanted to be a race car driver."

"See, then you could be like 'Aki the Flash,' since all the other drivers would only see your taillights."

Aki snickered into the glass and finished it off. "That's what they called me when I was in my motorcycle gang in high school."

"You like to drive fast, then?"

"Well, it's not like I can afford to get pulled over anymore, but before, I would drive so fast all the streetlights would blur."

"Sounds like fun."

Aki put the empty flute down, and Shinji filled it to the top, a few bubbles fizzing over. Shinji put his hand on Aki's thigh as he handed him back the drink, sending a lascivious tingling up Aki's spine. The alcoholic buzz must've had something to do with it. Shinji's hand lingered there a few seconds longer than necessary, and all of Aki's body grew hot.

A small moan leapt from the back of Aki's throat. His eyes

grew wide, and he coughed, hoping Shinji hadn't heard it, but Shinji's smile spoke otherwise.

"Watanabe said you were helping with the exchange," Aki quickly asked.

"My mother was Russian, so it helps when dealing with them, and I direct the videos with the girls after."

"Did you always want to direct porn?"

"Come on, do I really look that way?"

"Maybe a little."

Shinji ran his fingers through his hair, and Aki licked his lips at the way Shinji's muscles flexed. If his arms were that toned, the rest of him had to be ripped, too. Aki's skin tingled at the thought.

"I'm gonna have to walk around in a suit or something to get you to think better of me, huh?" Shinji laughed.

"Maybe."

"I want to direct real films one day. Something they'll show in every movie theater in Japan. Maybe even be good enough to show up in Hollywood."

"The Matsukawa actually own part of an indie film company that specializes in historic movies and the occasional yakuza film."

"Another reason why we should be allies." Shinji squeezed Aki's shoulder. "I'd love to see Kyoto sometime."

"It's the most beautiful city in all of Japan."

By the fourth champagne glass, Aki had almost forgotten about Nao. Shinji could be charming in his own way. He laid it on a bit thick, but with the lack of attention Aki had gotten, he really didn't mind someone being vocal with his attraction. It made his whole body warm thinking about it. Once he'd left high school, it felt like so much of his life was dedicated to trying to fit in.

"I was thinking…" Shinji casually draped his arm around Aki's shoulder. "Maybe we could go into—"

Aki shot up when Nao opened his door.

Nao didn't appear flushed, and his tie looked perfectly in place. It would be impossible to really know if he'd gone along with what Watanabe offered or if he'd really fucked the whore.

Aki gulped, getting trapped in one of Nao's glares.

He was fucked.

What was he thinking getting so drunk while at work?

Aki stumbled the first few steps but then met Nao as he strolled up to Watanabe in the center lounge.

"Was he to your liking?" Watanabe asked.

"It was interesting."

Nao grinned, and Aki's heart stopped. He really did have sex with the whore.

Watanabe laughed. "You'll buy my next batch from the Russians, then?"

"I need to think about it. You'll have my answer tomorrow."

"And here I thought we were friends."

Nao folded his arms. "Devils don't like going into deals they haven't set up. If you'd rather, I could make Aki look up flights back home for tonight."

"Tomorrow afternoon will be fine."

"I'm glad we can agree. Can one of your men get Kohta? He'll spend all night with those ladies if we let him."

Watanabe ordered one of the family members to carry out Nao's request. While they waited, Nao said nothing.

"Aki," Shinji called out. "Can I have your number?"

Aki's mouth grew dry. He looked back at Nao, who was waiting by the elevator. Aki rubbed his hands along his pants, then pulled out his phone. Nao would want him to be friendly toward their new allies, and it was smart to have Shinji's number, since he'd be at the exchange.

"Sure." Aki nodded.

Shinji held out his phone, and Aki typed in the number. Then Shinji called Aki.

"There we go. Now you have my number, too." He winked. "You call me if your boss lets you off the hook for a few hours. I'll show you a good time."

CHAPTER 6

•••

 **AO SIGHED AND** tapped his foot on the floorboard of the limo. Nothing about Hokkaido or the Mafufugumi impressed Nao. Not the Russian prostitute who barely knew three words of Japanese. Not the French restaurant that Nao had almost doubted carried sake. And definitely not Watanabe.

The Matsukawa were in no position to need impressing since they were the ones who'd asked about forming an alliance first. Still, five bars of gold for unlimited communication with Miko with a guarantee it wouldn't be monitored seemed too steep a price to ask. Surely the Matsukawa could bribe a guard for less money to slip communication, but the jail warden was Mafufugumi.

"Today is the last day of the snow festival," Aki said. "Perhaps seeing the sculptures will give us something more pleasing to remember about tonight."

Kohta held up his hands like a balancing act. "A bunch of snow or hot babes. I'll go with the babes."

"I'd like to see the sculptures," Nao said.

"Was your guy not good or something?"

Unlike Kohta, who was always too distracted by boobs to think with anything but his dick, Aki could always read whatever Nao was thinking, and he had an uncanny ability to pick the perfect tea to capture the day. Their shared morning pots of tea were one of the few times during the day-to-day as a godfather that Nao felt like himself.

"Maybe we can take a few of those ladies back to Kyoto with us?" Kohta asked.

Nao pinched the bridge of his nose, hoping it would stop the headache forming there. Aki tapped on the glass separating the limo and told the driver of their destination change.

Kohta glanced toward Aki. "That Shinji guy was checking you out."

Aki's cheeks pinkened, and he shifted in his seat. "I don't know what you mean."

"Come on, anyone with eyes could see he thought you were smoking hot."

"There was nothing of the sort."

"I know you're not oblivious. I've seen you flirt with guys when I took you out for your birthday. So did you head to the back with Shin—"

Nao cleared his throat, grinding his back teeth together.

"Let's not talk about that here." Nao gestured to the driver.

Kohta nodded. "Right, Boss."

There could be microphones all over the limo. The driver probably had instructions to report back to Watanabe with the nature of their conversation.

Nao tilted his head toward Aki. "Before we leave, grab Watanabe's home address, along with his headquarters'. We'll take our own taxi."

"Understood."

Aki pulled out his phone, the blue light painting his face in a heavy glow that accentuated his large eyes and rounded cheeks. He was no doubt comparing the different taxi services, checking out customers' reviews and cross-checking it with the company's policies on yakuza.

Nao couldn't have picked a better secretary, which was why he'd wanted to punch Shinji until his eyes swelled shut for the way he'd looked at Aki. Like at any moment Shinji was ready to pounce on Aki, tie him to the nearest bed, and lap at every centimeter of his skin just to hear the different moans he'd make.

Nao crossed his legs. Aki deserved someone better than a porn director.

No.

Aki could have anyone he wanted. Nao didn't care, because if he cared, Kyoto would find a way to kill Aki. Kyoto had found some way to murder everyone he'd ever cared about.

Shinya…

Even Saehyun…

Nao bit his cheek and looked away from Aki.

Aki could fuck or fall in love with whomever he wanted as long as it wasn't him.

"Has Kurosawa called yet?" Nao asked.

Aki shook his head.

"Hey, no news is good news, right?" Kohta said.

Nao crossed his arms. "I don't like that he hasn't checked in. I have a bad feeling."

"I'll call when we get out."

A pain welled in Nao's chest like a thousand strings were tugging on him at once back to Kyoto. It was wrong to be gone so far away from the city that needed him. Nao stayed silent, letting the pain be a reminder of how the important alliance with the Mafufugumi needed to be sealed quickly.

Kohta took the quiet as an opportunity to speak about the dish he ate at the awful French place the rest of the ride. Aki even joined in speaking about his distaste for his cod but his enjoyment of the bread. Slowly they'd built up a kind of working friendship since Kohta had joined the Matsukawa. They were stuck together wherever Nao went, so it was good they were becoming friends.

The limo pulled over, and the driver let them out. He mentioned taking their luggage to their destination for them.

Once the limo was out of sight, Aki pulled out his phone. "Do you want to speak with Kurosawa, or would you rather I deal with the phone?"

Nao hated the device, which was why he forced Aki to carry it around for him. The ache in his chest compelled him to hold out his hand to accept the device. Aki pulled up the number and called before passing it over.

"Hello, Hisona, what's going on?" Kurosawa said.

Nao frowned. "Is everything okay back home?"

"Oh, pardon me, Father Murata, I didn't realize it was you.

Everything is quiet here."

"Are you sure?" Nao paced. "I have a bad feeling. Like all of this is the calm before the storm."

"No, I got the check from the ward leaders a few hours ago, and there was no sign of the Koreans."

"I want you to check in with Aki at least every four hours."

"Father Murata, that seems—"

"I don't care if everything is as perfect as a spring stroll down the Philosopher's Path. I want to be kept informed."

"Yes. I'll make sure to do that."

"Good."

Nao handed the phone back to Aki, who hung it up and slipped it back into his pocket.

"You feelin' better?" Kohta asked, lighting up a cigarette.

The crisp air filled Nao's lungs, and even though a tug still pulled inside of him, it had dulled with the phone call.

They strolled through the park, gazing at the different snow sculptures. They weren't as impressive as any of the grand floats of Kyoto's Gion festival. The only thing grand about Sapporo was the temperature difference and all the snow.

"It's horrible how the *Star Wars* snow float is more popular than the traditional palace," Nao said, gazing up at the sculpture. "The lack of tradition in Sapporo is disappointing."

Kohta stared at the temple made of snow and tapped the ashes off his cigarette. "It was kind of cool to see a white Darth Vader."

"The lack of appreciation for Japanese culture explains how Watanabe can so easily work with those filthy Russians."

Aki nodded along, the first flurries of snow falling onto his black hair. Nao was really fit for the yakuza. Sure, when he'd been pushed, he'd attacked, but even a mouse would strike a snake when confronted. Would Shinji be waiting for Aki at the Mafufugumi headquarters? Nao had caught them exchanging numbers. Had they planned to meet again later tonight?

"Should I change our tickets home?" Aki asked, the air fogging around him. "I had us leaving tomorrow afternoon after your visit with Miko, but if we get the prostitutes, we might have to adjust the schedule?"

Nao pressed his lips together. Logic urged him to go ahead and sink to Watanabe's demand, but an unsettling feeling had loomed over him since the moment he'd stepped foot in Sapporo. He needed to get home.

"Don't change it yet," Nao said. "What float do you like best?"

"The temple is really breathtaking."

Nao ran his fingers through his hair. "It's too bad we haven't tried the curry soup. I heard it's a popular Sapporo dish."

Aki had hinted about the dish when he'd bought their plane tickets for the trip.

"Perhaps if Watanabe doesn't take us out for lunch, we can eat there."

"That does sound good." Nao resisted the urge to squeeze Aki's shoulder and shoved his hands into his pockets.

Nao looked away, keeping his attention to the snow hood of Vader. "When you two stay at Mafufugumi headquarters, keep an eye out. See if you notice anything off. I don't trust anyone that would look outside Japan for an ally."

"We are going ahead with the new deal, then, Boss?" Kohta asked.

"Watanabe has us by the balls with this one. Before the Koreans strike, we need to establish a clear line of communication with Miko." Nao shook his head. "I'm surprised they haven't already launched an attack as it is. Five bars of gold is so steep though."

Kohta smashed his spent cigarette on the bottom of his shoe. "They were really good if that's any help."

Nao glanced toward Aki. "See if you can get in contact with Jun before we visit Miko tomorrow. Ask if he knew about the trade with the Russians."

"I won't fail you, Father Murata," Aki said.

"You'd think Watanabe would have Jun out by now. Something doesn't feel right. Everything that's happened since we came has been tipping more and more into Watanabe's favor. He already had the upper hand in this deal. I can imagine tomorrow he'd think of some new way to fuck us over some more."

Kohta laughed. "Are you sure it's not your usual paranoia?"

"It's kept me alive so far. Do your jobs, and tomorrow, report to me the lies you're able to sniff out."

CHAPTER 7

AKI CROSSED HIS arms. "We have to share a room?"

"Sorry, we don't have any extra space." The Mafufugumi gave a light bow of his head. "This is the best room in the place since it has the connecting bathroom."

Kohta plopped his suitcase on the bed farther away from the door. "No worries. Thanks for shuffling everyone so we could get this much. I know it's no fun bunking up with new people."

"Just tell me if you need anything."

"You guys up for a few rounds of cards?" Kohta asked.

"Sure, I'll go see if the other guys want to play."

"You got beer in the fridge?"

"Should be."

"Then I'll meet everyone there."

The Mafufugumi left Kohta and Aki in the small room. The two Western-style twin beds took up most of the space. The rough blue sheets were too starched for Aki's liking, but at least they were clean. If they'd used traditional futons, like the Matsukawa, Aki would've simply moved his bed somewhere else. Anyone would be better than Kohta.

Aki crossed his arms. "We were supposed to be searching for information, not goofing off."

"People let stuff slip when they play cards, especially when they're tipsy."

Kohta threw his coat on his bed and dug through the explosion of color that was his suitcase. He opened his suitcase and tossed various items onto his bed. After a few seconds he stopped, unbuttoned his shirt, and put on one just as gaudy but with dogs and a golden mask on it.

"Do you like it?" He asked.

"No."

"Must be jealous then. You know I'd let you borrow something if you asked."

"Don't worry, I'm not."

Kohta shook his head. "Why not? Maybe that's why you didn't find someone at that club I took you to on your birthday. All you wore was black. No one could spot you."

"I didn't want to go in the first place."

Kohta's shoulders slumped. "I wanted to see what you looked like when you finally loosened up. You can't work twenty-four seven even if Boss acts like we can."

"It's our duty—"

"I know, I know." Kohta waved his hand in front of him. "To uphold Nao and the Matsukawa family. You're like a robot sometimes. When was the last time you remember having any fun?"

Aki had nothing he wanted to say to Kohta, and if he carried on, Kohta would've continued chatting. Though, Kohta would probably talk to a wall if no one else was there. Eventually he pushed his hair over his shoulder and squeezed passed Aki to the door.

Kohta smiled. "You sure you don't want to take a breather and join one game?"

"As sure as I am about never wanting to borrow your clothes."

"Your loss then."

The door slammed behind Kohta, and Aki plopped onto his bed. He shouldn't have to be the one who did all the work, but again he was. He loosened his tie before pulling it over his head and undoing the first few buttons of his white dress shirt.

Aki waited until the card game was in full swing before poking his head out the door. While the Matsukawa head-quarters housed several jumpsuit-wearing new recruits, the Mafufugumi seemed to have none. Another tradition they'd let go. Though Aki wouldn't have minded his time not wearing his, but it made a clear distinction of seniority.

He strolled down the hallways and into the kitchen. Most of the products there were low quality and reminded Aki of what his high school friends would steal from the convenience store before riding off on their bikes.

"Thanks. It's from the latest Versace season."

Aki's gaze darted to the sound of Kohta's voice coming from the living room. Someone actually complimented his clothes? Nao was right, something couldn't be right with them.

Aki cleared the rest of the first floor and climbed the carpeted stairs up to the second. The layout felt more like a residential home than a yakuza headquarters. They might've not housed the new recruits underneath the watchful eye of their seniors, which struck Aki as odd. Most yakuza were rebellious teens and needed the discipline of tending to the domestic duties of keeping the headquarters cleaned and preparing meals to determine who could really hack it in the strict hierarchy of yakuza.

The hallways grew tighter in the second story, and light flooded from the bottom of the many doorways. The voices from one came a little louder than the others, and Aki strolled over and leaned beside the door. He pulled out his phone and pulled up a note app in case anything worthwhile came up.

"If they don't do it then we're screwed," one voice inside said.

Aki narrowed his eyes. They had to be talking about the Matsukawa.

"They don't have a choice," another voice spoke up.

"But you saw how mad he was."

Their voices continued but grew softer. Aki pressed himself against the door, straining to hear more.

"Who knows what's really going on."

"Watanabe seemed confident…"

A large Mafufugumi stood beside Aki and cleared his throat. He stood a head taller than Aki and wore a frown that meant business.

"I'm Aki Hisona from the Matsukawa." Aki smiled and politely bowed. "We're so thankful for such generosity on our stay in Sapporo."

"You a cocksucker like your boss." He spat.

"Excuse me?"

The guy leaned forward, hunching over until he was eye-to-eye with Aki. "You got lips like a cocksucker. So you must be a cocksucker."

"Screw you."

Aki tried to step away, but the man slammed his hand against the wall, blocking Aki's escape.

He grabbed Aki's collar. "You must be waiting until they're finished so you can get those pouty lips of yours around one."

Aki balled his fingers into a fist, and his phone vibrated in his pocket. The guy had height and weight on his side, but Aki wasn't going to back down. He needed to end the fight quickly so he could answer the phone. Aki ducked down and then slammed the top of his head on the Mafufugumi's throat. He staggered back and hugged the wall as he coughed.

"I might be a cocksucker, but I can still kick your ass," Aki yelled.

He pulled his phone from his pocket and watched the man stagger off. At least he wasn't going to mess with Aki the rest of the night. The vibration brought Aki's attention back to his phone.

Kurosawa.

It couldn't be good.

"This is Hisona," Aki said, walking back into his bedroom.

Kurosawa's voice came on the line. "I need to speak to Nao,"

"He's not here. Give me a few a seconds, and I can give you the number of where he's staying."

"Why aren't you with him?"

Aki closed the bedroom door behind him and stood in the bathroom to keep anyone from being able to listen outside the door. Then he explained the situation about the hotels rejecting them to Kurosawa. Then the added condition Watanabe demanded before sealing off the alliance.

"This isn't good," Kurosawa said.

"I think Father Murata is waiting to speak with Miko to make his final decision."

"Good choice on his part."

Aki nodded, refolding one of the washcloths that had been set out for them. "What's going on at home? Do you need the number where Nao is staying? I need to get him. I have the address and can be there soon."

Kurosawa sighed. "It doesn't really matter now. I was making a final call before heading to bed."

"What do you mean now?"

"A few hours back, three Korean mob members were desecrating the Toyokuni shrine by spreading oil on the boards. We caught them but turned them over to the police. It wasn't like they fired at one of our safehouses."

Aki pressed. "But it was Toyokuni shrine. Is—"

"Those Korean bastards were doing the same thing as when they tried to go after the Gion floats last time. It's nothing major, and the situation is already taken care of."

"But—"

"Murata needs to focus on getting the alliance with Watanabe finished. We can't even conduct the war without a clear line of communication with Miko. So it would be silly to distract him."

Aki tapped his thumb against the bathroom counter. Kurosawa wasn't listening. That shrine had been built to commemorate Toyotomi Hideyoshi, the daimyo who went to war with Korea. It also stood next to the Mimizuka, where the tens of thousands of Koreans' ears and noses had been stacked as a war trophy then buried in a knoll. It happened in the 1500s and stood forgotten about by most Japanese, but to every Korean, it stood for a reminder of Japanese cruelty. It would be the very symbol the Korean mob would use to declare their intent.

"Are you even listening?" Kurosawa yelled.

"Sorry."

"What did I say then?"

Aki swallowed.

"Get your head out of your ass," Kurosawa said.

"But wouldn't it be something he needs to know? I won't have to tell him right now, but when I see him—"

"No."

"But Father Murata would want to know. You called and asked for him, so you had intended to tell him."

"Hisona, listen to me." Kurosawa paused for a few seconds. "Are you listening?"

Aki pressed his fist into the counter. Kurosawa took every opportunity to humiliate him whenever Nao wasn't around.

"Yes," Aki said, his tone flat.

"Open up your ears and remember where you stand in this family. How fucking dare you question me? You're a secretary. You haven't even been a full-fledged member for more than a year. You are dog shit! I'm giving you a direct order, Hisona. Do not tell Murata anything about this phone call. If you do, you'll be stuck burning bodies for the rest of your sad existence. I don't care how much Murata likes looking at your ass. Understood?"

"Understood."

"Good."

"Homophobic bastard," Aki mumbled, hanging up the phone.

Aki buried his hands over his face, imagining all the horrible things Kurosawa would make up about him to force Nao to dismiss him. If he wanted to stay by Nao's side, Aki had to follow the orders.

Aki took out his contacts and bathed. The hot water surrounding him helped soothe his thoughts. He stayed soaking in the tub until the water turned cold. He slipped into bed, but there it was just as difficult to escape his thoughts. He'd fade between dreaming and awareness like a half-realized dream. The sound of laughter would carry to the door then subside.

The blue screen of Aki's phone woke him. He reached for it, half expecting it to be Shinji, but it was just a weather alert about the snow. Aki groaned. It was two in the morning. If Shinji really wanted to be with him, Aki had expected some kind of late-night call asking him to go out or at least an invite asking him to his place.

Aki rolled over, covering his bare shoulder with the rough sheets. He pressed his hand against the wall. Without sleeping in the room beside Nao, it felt too strange to sleep. Aki's fingers trailed down his chest, and he pressed his palm on his crotch. He'd lost count of the times he'd jacked off thinking of how only a thin wall had separated him from Nao. Aki palmed his crotch more thinking of all the times Nao and he had pretended to have sex so Nao could sneak out. How Nao had felt him up and said how it was highly inappropriate that Aki had sported a hard-on during their charade. His favorite fantasy turned Nao's smile into something wicked, and instead of leaving, he'd stayed to punish Aki for his indiscretion. The whole house would hear his screams of pleasure, and for once they wouldn't have been fake.

Damn.

He was hard.

Of course, he was imagining the top ten pleasure-seeking punishments Nao would serve him. Aki pushed the covers off and exposed his half-hard cock to the cold air. It prickled his skin with a luscious delight. He closed his eyes, imagining Nao's hand replacing his as it ever so slowly wrapped around the base of his dick. His fantasy picked back up, but somehow it wasn't as vivid as back home. Knowing that Nao was so far away killed the mood. That was another fantasy. How one day Nao would come in and finish Aki off for him without saying a word.

Aki sighed, opening his eyes and slowing down his pace. The only person he'd been with since joining the yakuza was his right hand. It was pathetic.

Maybe he should call Shinji. Considering all the flirting, he'd probably be up for a late-night sex call. Aki smirked. He could even send him a picture of his cock, and he probably would jump at the idea.

Aki buried his head in his pillow. How pathetic was he? He didn't want a picture of his dick floating out there for everyone to see. He'd just have to finish himself off.

His fingers trailed down his cock, and he thumbed the head, spreading the pre-cum there. Maybe if he'd been more forward, Shinji would've screwed him in the bathroom. He could've bent Aki over the counter and dropped his pants right there. Aki's toes curled at the thought as he picked up his rhythm. Would Shinji take Aki, barely prep him, and then watch his face contort in the mirror before them?

Two of Aki's fingers slipped into this mouth, and he coated them with saliva. Shinji could show him what those muscles of his could do. Aki opened his legs, imagining taking all of Shinji into him. Aki's fingers trailed down his tight abs and to the place he needed it most.

"Oh shit!" Kohta called.

Aki quickly covered himself with the blanket.

"Fuck, man," Kohta continued, not moving from his spot holding open the door. "Haven't you heard of putting a sock on the doorknob?"

Aki fled to the bathroom. He turned on the cold water and splashed some on his red face. His whole face was red.

"I'm sorry, I wasn't thinking about…"

"No worries, man, everyone does it. I was just surprised. Why didn't you call that Shinji guy? He would've helped you with that."

"I don't want to talk about it."

Kohta laughed. "I'm glad to know you find some way to get the stress out."

Aki groaned. Any kind of arousal he had was gone, and it

sure as fuck wasn't going to happen with Kohta in the room.

"You can shut up now," Aki said.

Kohta sighed, and once silence came from the other side of the door, Aki opened it. Kohta was there right beside the door, his arms crossed.

"I know I'll never hear the end of this, but it would be nice if we could just keep this to ourselves," Aki said.

Kohta shook his head. "I'm not that bad."

"Yeah, you are."

"I've only tried to be friends with you. I took you out on your birthday—"

"I didn't want to go."

"But you had a little fun. I saw you dance."

"It's late," Aki said. "I just want to go to sleep."

"Look, what I want to say is, even if you don't believe me, I've got your back. Even if you don't, I consider you my friend on top of just being members of the same family. What can I do to prove it to you? Because so far all my stuff I learned as a host hasn't worked on you."

Aki raised a brow. "Are you serious?"

Kohta put his hand over his heart. "As serious as my love for Versace."

"Then for us to be friends, you need to cut your hair, maybe dye it too."

"Wait. What? You don't like my hair?"

Aki crossed his arms over his chest. He knew Kohta's offer was too good to be true. "Yeah, I hate it. Blond doesn't suit you at all."

"Done."

"You really mean it?"

"Once I get back home and Boss gives me the day off, I'll chop it all off for you."

Aki smiled. "Thanks."

"I can come back in ten minutes if you need to finish up."

"The mood's already dead. We should get some sleep. Father Murata talks to Miko for the first time tomorrow, so he'll probably be more on edge than usual."

"You know him so well."

Aki crawled into bed. "Not as well as I want to."

CHAPTER 8

❖❖❖

THE HIGH FENCE and gray building made Nao's limbs tingle like they had back when he served his time at the juvenile detention center. He'd broken the arm of a kid in three places, but the kid had deserved it for calling his father nothing but a glorified meat packer. Nao had managed to avoid incarceration since then.

Yet as Nao stood outside, waiting for Aki and Kohta to slide out of the limo, the tingling in his limbs turned into a thousand needles piercing his skin. The last time he'd seen Miko, she'd scolded him as bad as when his father had banished him from the family.

The limo pulled away, and Nao cleared his throat, but it only alleviated some of the pressure.

"What did you find at the Mafufugumi's headquarters?" Nao asked.

Kohta laughed and shook his head. "There was no need to worry, Boss. They were nice guys. Welcomed us with a big party.

I got so drunk I even lost a game of cards."

"You were supposed to be looking for anything suspicious."

"Well, they didn't poison us. So that's good."

Nao rubbed his temple. He let Kohta get away with too much and needed to make it stop before he looked like a total failure of a godfather.

"Please tell me you did better, Aki?" Nao asked.

Aki's eyes softened when Nao used his first name. Nao knew he should've dropped the habit when it became clear Aki had feelings for him. Still, the last name Hisona had never matched Aki's gentle nature.

"I heard some people worried that you wouldn't accept the deal," Aki started. "And for the amount of men residing there, they didn't have nearly as much food as required, and what they had was cheap quality, but they might've been receiving a delivery soon."

"Or they don't give a crap about their recruits," Kohta said.

"At least Aki was trying to do his job and not partying with traitors to Japan who still aren't our allies," Nao said.

"Come on, Boss, people let things slip when they're drunk."

"Hopefully you didn't."

"I'm always professional."

Aki laughed. "Do you see what you're wearing?"

"This is Versace."

"It looks like it was designed in the dark."

Nao sighed as Aki and Kohta went back and forth. What disturbed Nao was more the fact he was shown nothing but hospitality at Watanabe's house as well. He was minutes away from speaking with Miko because of some sinking suspicion. He had no evidence to show.

"You're lucky Father Murata hasn't put you on a dress code." Aki crossed his arms. "Oh, there's one thing a bit strange but not related to the Mafufugumi. Unfortunately, I've still been unable to get in contact with Jun. I called the police but was put on hold. They eventually hung up, and when I called back, I got the same results."

Nao narrowed his eyes. "Watanabe assured me Jun would be out before we left for home. The exchange should be over before evening, so this isn't good. And what about home? Have the Koreans done anything in my absence?"

Aki rubbed his palm with his thumb. "Kurosawa called earlier and said everything was running smoothly."

"I only hope it's not the quiet before the storm." Nao took a few steps toward the prison entry, but Aki stayed put. "Was there something else?"

"I asked the new recruits to send photos." Aki pressed his lips together and held out the phone. "She meowed at the door for hours after you left."

A smile crossed Nao's face. The picture was of Nobu, his hairless black cat, reaching for the front door handle, her skin wrinkling on her legs and back.

"Hopefully we won't have to make her wait much longer," Nao said.

They checked in through the main gate, and a slender man with a large mustache greeted them. Other than the facial hair, the man was forgettable, but it made him perfect as a member of the Mafufugumi working within the system.

"You're Mr. Murata?" he asked.

Nao nodded.

"I'm the warden here. We have a friend in common."

"I hope at least."

"This way. I got everything you need already taken care of."

The warden escorted them down a taupe hallway and to an area littered with posters about visitation rules. A single door stood in the middle of the hallway, and a window in it showed Miko already waiting at a table for him.

"No one will be listening or watching," the warden said.

They were lucky to get the meeting without the alliance formalized.

Nao stepped inside the visitation room, leaving Aki and Kohta outside. Four tables dotted the room, and a camera was mounted on the wall. A few moments after Nao entered, the red button on the camera turned off.

Cigarette smoke curled around Miko. Her long black hair framed her face. Even in the orange jumpsuit, one look from her sent a shiver down Nao's spine. His father had been right to select her as godfather. She'd been his right-hand man for as long as Nao could remember.

Nao gave a formal bow, while Miko nodded. Nao took off his coat and covered the back of the plastic chair while Miko took another puff of her cigarette.

"Being in a place like this must bring back memories," she said.

Nao gave a faint smile and sat in a chair. "Mostly ones I want forgotten."

"You look different without the yukata."

"They didn't seem fitting for the Matsukawa boss to wear. Though maybe I should wear tracksuits to blend in better."

Miko laughed. "I see you've met our Tokyo and Osaka allies."

"Renewing their alliances was the first order of business."

"It must've been interesting."

Nao swallowed. "What do you mean?"

"Seeing you drink sake with an ally we almost went to war with over that pointless rampage of yours." She shook her head and tapped the ash off her cigarette. "I still don't know how your father negotiated us out of a war after what you did on your little excursion with what's-his-name."

"His name was Shinya." Nao swallowed, but his throat remained dry.

She leaned back and took a long drag. "But I guess that evening did start the legend of Nao Murata."

Nao understood why Miko was dragging up the biggest of Nao's failures. She was making sure Nao understood his place, but it didn't make the gut-wrenching feeling stab him any less. He might be godfather to everyone else, but to her, Nao was still the rebellious teen.

"I knew making you active godfather until I got back was the right decision. Sakai wouldn't even have the guts to order someone to rip out the tongue of our enemy, and you'd do that without a second thought. The Matsukawa is in good hands with you."

"It's a humbling honor to serve the family in your absence."

Smoke drifted around her. "The alliance with the Mafufugumi is going along nicely. It's all finished?"

Nao's hand clenched into a fist. "That bastard Watanabe suddenly changed the terms of the agreement."

"What does he want us to cough up?"

"He wants us to finish some deal he started with the Russians. It infuriates me he so easily goes back on his word."

Miko blew out a line of smoke. "It shows how much of a neophyte you are to this. It's not uncommon to make last-minute demands. We're the ones with everything to gain. You would probably do the same thing."

"I'd never work with a foreign mob. The Russians are as bad as the Koreans."

"Come now, be sensible." Miko leaned back in her chair with a turned-up lip. "I'm going to be stuck here the next five years. We need that line of communication. The Mafufugumi are the only ones who can do it."

"I don't trust him! Too many things aren't adding up."

"Nao, you're not good at diplomacy."

Nao blinked. "I—"

Miko held up her hand, and her eyes narrowed. "That was a statement. I knew the Matsukawa would be safe *from the Koreans* with you as a leader. But when it comes to being subtle or dealing with the day-to-day, you need to leave it to Sakai and Kurosawa."

The words pulled at Nao's core like Miko had thrust a sword into him and slowly ripped out his intestines one centimeter at a time. Nao closed his eyes, but it only intensified the pain. Still, he knew everything Miko said was true. During the quiet days around headquarters, Nao's melancholy drew him inward, and he would slip into numbness. It sometimes faded after a few days and other times would stretch on for weeks. Even Aki's tea couldn't wake him. Could he only ever be the Nao who slaughtered men?

Nao pressed his fist into the table. "But I know something isn't right."

"You're still so young." Miko reached out, grasping Nao's hand in hers, and put on a gentle smile. "You don't understand how things work."

"But I can feel it! In my heart I know something isn't right. Every second here, it hurts more."

"When was the last time you stepped outside of Kyoto for more than a couple of hours?"

Nao bit his tongue. She knew the answer.

"What happened that time?" she asked. "What happened when you started overthinking then?"

She clutched Nao's hand. He tried to pull away, but she kept her grip on tight. He held his breath, but Shinya's scream echoed in his eyes.

His voice lowered. "It's been a while."

"Your nerves are getting the best of you. It's time to grow up and think."

"But—"

Miko groaned and jerked Nao's hand over, exposing his wrist. His eyes widened, but before he could defend himself, she smashed the cigarette onto Nao's wrist. He yelped.

"Are you even listening?" she snapped, keeping her viselike grip on Nao's wrist. "Everyone has something going on. What matters is if it's big enough to stop what they can do for us. I can guarantee you it's not."

She released Nao's wrist, and he jerked it back, tossing lingering black ash on the floor. A red circular lesion pulsed on his wrist, and an almost electric heat ran through his whole arm. Nao curled his fingers into a fist as a light sting pulsed on his wrist. A red circle formed around the center black hole.

"Wouldn't it be better to discover what the dirt actually is?" he shouted.

"If you want to, fine, but I don't care if they spat on the emperor's grave. We're going ahead." She nodded to Nao's wrist. "Keep that as a reminder of your place. You lose all control when you're outside the city. We don't need a bloodbath, we need an alliance."

A knock came on the door, and Nao looked back. The warden held up two fingers, signaling the two minutes remaining before the cameras turned back on.

Miko slipped the pack of cigarettes back into her jumpsuit. "Don't fuck this up, Nao. I know you'll do the Matsukawa proud."

"Of course." Nao's jaw clenched.

When Nao left, Kohta and Aki were chatting—well, it was mostly Kohta chatting and Aki rubbing a thumb over the back of his hand. Had he left all his paper back in Kyoto? He'd always spent every spare second at home folding cranes.

"That's just a taste of what the alliance between our families can provide you," the warden said.

"The sampling was much appreciated," Nao replied.

The rest of the walk out of the prison was in silence. Nao's thoughts raced. He had no choice. He never had a choice. He was at the mercy of whatever Miko needed.

Once they got outside, Nao stopped. Aki and Kohta looked up to him as their godfather. None of the older Matsukawa looked at him the way they and the newer recruits did. They needed him. He could be the godfather. Miko would see. Nao clutched his wrist. He'd find out what was going on even if Miko didn't see the need.

"Aki, get the gold," Nao said. "Kohta, go back to the Mafufugumi headquarters and see if your poker buddies have anything they want to complain about. There's some dirt these guys are hiding, and I want to know before we drink sake with them."

CHAPTER 9

WITH HOW DIFFICULT it had proved in getting a hotel room, Aki expected the guards to knock him flat on his face when he stepped outside the bank with the briefcase of cash. Aki shook his head. Nao's paranoia must've rubbed off on him. Whatever the case, it still made Aki look like the most incompetent secretary in the world.

Businessmen weaved in and out around Aki's slow walk before he eventually plopped down on a bench.

He rubbed his eyes and yawned. Staying at Watanabe's headquarters and not the room next to Nao left Aki's dreams corrupted with nightmares of Nao and that Russian whore instead of fantasies of Nao. Then Shinji would step in and turn it into a wet dream.

No matter how Aki wished it, he couldn't change the past. He needed to focus on exchanging the cash for gold so Nao wouldn't be stuck with Kohta for company all day. But most

pawn shops wouldn't take a briefcase of cash without raising an eyebrow.

Aki pulled out his phone and thumbed through the contacts. Shinji would know which pawn shop would be yakuza friendly.

Aki called.

"Hey," Shinji said after a few rings.

"This is Aki Hisona. We met last night."

"There's no way I could forget you."

Aki tilted his head and cleared his throat. "I need to know the name of a friendly pawn shop. Do you have any recommendations?"

"It's nice to hear your voice again, Aki."

Did Shinji really have to use his first name?

"If you could give me the address, then I won't have to disturb you anymore," Aki said.

"Disturb? No, I'm happy that you called. I was hoping you'd call last night."

Shinji's deep voice lulled in Aki's ear. Aki's skin grew hot as the memory of a dream flashed before him. Shinji had pinned him against the bathroom counter and was pounding into him. He'd pull at Aki's hair, whispering for him to watch how he looked. Shinji had clutched onto him so hard it left bruises. A hard and erotic fuck just like Aki wanted it.

Aki licked his lips and pushed down the dream. "I really need to get this taken care of soon," Aki said.

"Where are you?"

"Outside Nippon Bank."

"I'll be there in ten minutes."

"You don't need—"

Shinji hung up, leaving Aki no option but to wait. He ran his fingers through his hair, but a little part of him was excited to see the man again. Hopefully they'd leave for Kyoto soon. He didn't want to turn into Kohta and only think about his dick during work.

While he waited, Aki called the jail. He'd been placed on hold for five minutes before the line died. Then he checked in back home—everything was fine—and ordered one of the house recruits to send over a few more photos of the cat. He'd tried to make a crane with the bank receipt, but the wind was blowing too hard to try after the first few folds.

A car's engine accelerating pulled Aki's attention away from the phone. His eyes grew wide as a red Ferrari 458 pulled up in front of him. The sculpted body and raised headlights on the fenders sent a shiver down Aki's spine. He was in love.

The door opened, and Shinji stepped out wearing tight black jeans and a red plaid coat with a few more zippers than necessary to give it a rocker vibe. But that car!

"You like it?" Shinji asked, gesturing to the sweetest ride Aki had been able to get close to in a long time.

"Like it?" Aki ran his hand across the warm hood. "I'm ready to propose."

Shinji leaned over beside Aki and tapped the hood. "She does have one hell of a purr when she's hot."

Shinji's red jacket rode up and revealed jeans hugging his ass like a second skin. He was showing off, but at the same time, Aki didn't mind. If Nao could sleep with some Russian bastard, Aki could stare at the ass of an attractive guy with an even hotter car.

"You want to drive?" Shinji tossed the keys to Aki, who caught them in one hand.

"You mean it?"

"I don't tease—at least not outside the bedroom."

No other keys ever felt like they belonged in his hand. Aki shoved the briefcase in the back and slid into the driver's seat. He brushed his hands over the fine leather detail. His fingers were made for the steering wheel.

"I always wanted to drive something like this."

Shinji got beside him. "Murata doesn't let you drive his flashy cars?"

Aki laughed. "Domestic brands aren't known for their looks."

"Jun told us he didn't buy things not made by Japanese companies, but I didn't believe him."

"It's true—everything from cars to suits. The only foreign thing he touches is his tea."

"And a good hooker."

Aki slammed on the gas, peeling out onto the street.

"Show-off." Shinji grinned.

Aki asked, "Where's the pawn shop?"

Shinji grabbed on to the door and let out a small laugh. "Good thing we have a deal with the cops."

"Really? I've had a hard time getting ahold of Jun."

"You have to ask the right person."

"I see. Who's the right person?"

"I forgot his name since I just deal with our Russia allies."

Aki floored the accelerator, speeding through a changing light.

"Father Murata is disappointed he hasn't been released yet."

"Don't worry. We don't want to raise suspicion. He'll be released by the time we get back from the exchange with the Russians."

More like get done holding Jun hostage. Nao was right. Something was off about the whole trip.

Aki slowed to a stop at a red light. The engine purred as if crying to be set free. Sports cars weren't meant to be stuck idling.

Shinji pointed. "It'll be a right at the next light."

Shinji's hair fell in his eyes, and he swept it back. Even with the coat, his biceps bulged. Nao kept his muscles lean, refining them in a boxing ring rather than lifting weights like Shinji must've done to get them so large.

Aki licked his lips. Both were appealing in their own way. Shinji probably would look hotter pinning Aki's hands above his head and would have much more power behind each of his slamming thrusts. He could imagine the marks left on his back from being banged against the wall. Shinji could mark his body anyway he wanted. A small moan left the back of Aki's throat, and if Shinji had heard it, he thankfully didn't react, but Aki's body had.

He blamed it on the car and the way it vibrated when they stopped. Not the fact that Shinji was objectively the hottest guy who'd ever hit on him before. Aki hadn't just imagined what sex with him would be like for a full light change.

The light switched to green and Aki peeled out, hoping it would distract Shinji enough not to notice the bulge growing in Aki's trousers.

CHAPTER 10

TRADING THE BRIEFCASE filled with money for the gold went as smoothly as when Aki picked up paper from his favorite stationery store.

Snow fluttered from the sky as Aki and Shinji stepped out of the shop. Aki pulled his coat collar a little closer. He should've brought a scarf with him, but it was impossible to have known he wouldn't be on the flight back home before the weather turned.

"Thanks again for showing me a friendly place," Aki said.

Shinji smiled. "Since we're here, why don't we go to an onsen? Hokkaido has the best hot springs."

"Father Murata wishes to return home as quickly as possible. I need to get the gold back so we can begin the trade."

"It doesn't matter if you leave now."

Aki narrowed his eyes. "What?"

Shinji held up a finger. "There's only one train to the village where the deals take place. It leaves in the morning and doesn't make the return trip until four. So we have hours before we can leave to meet it."

It sounded like an excuse Shinji had made up in order to get him naked at an onsen. Aki licked his lips. Sure, he wouldn't mind seeing Shinji naked, too, but not at the expense of delaying his duty to Nao.

"You direct porn movies for the Mafufugumi," Aki said. "How do you know anything about the exchange?"

"Ouch." Shinji put a hand over his chest. "That one hurt."

"I didn't mean any disrespect by say—"

"Sounded like you did."

Snow covered Aki's polished shoes and Shinji's boots.

"Sorry," Aki said. "Since leaving Kyoto, Father Murata has been more on edge. It makes me want to please him more."

"But it's wrong to take it out on me."

Shinji bent over to reach for something in the car. He wiggled a little, almost as if to make sure Aki was checking him out. Oh, and he was. How could he not? With one final wiggle, Shinji pulled out a black umbrella. He opened it with a quick snap and held it over Aki's head.

"You were getting snow in your hair." Shinji brushed off a few of the flakes.

Aki shook his head, and snow fluttered down. Shinji chuckled and brushed some of them off Aki's shoulder.

"There. I think we got them all." Shinji smiled.

"But your hair's covered now."

"I take after my mom. It's going to get frizzy the second we enter the onsen anyway."

"So your mother was Russian?"

"Yeah." Shinji rubbed his neck.

Aki smiled, hoping to help ease Shinji's thoughts about being a mix. "I'm fluent in Korean for similar reasons."

"My film studio is where the exchanges always take place. We always get the movies with the girls filmed first before shipping them off here. So I'll be stuck there for a while after I get there. I'd like to enjoy a nice Sapporo bath before I leave."

"Couldn't we drive to the exchange? It would save a lot of time."

Shinji laughed. "The village gets at least a meter of snow a year, and last week, they had a huge storm. They close the roads this time of year because it's so dangerous. The train is the only way in and out, and we're lucky since they just dug it out from the last storm, but if it keeps snowing like this…"

"Seems like a bad location."

"What? No. It's a wonderful location. The cops never bother us, and we don't have to bribe them like we do here." Shinji twirled the umbrella, sending a flurry of snowflakes down. "So is that a yes to an onsen?"

"I don't want to leave the gold somewhere not safe."

"The lockers are right next to the bath. So the briefcase will never be out of your sight. When was the last time you did something for yourself and not for Murata? Don't work yourself to death. Even Kohta got to have some fun."

Aki grabbed the handle of the umbrella, his pinkie brushing against Shinji's. "Only if you hold the umbrella over both of us. I'm not some princess."

Shinji smiled and stepped under. "Of course not. You're a prince."

Aki turned his head, his cheeks growing hot. "Don't say that."

"Why not, Your Highness?" Shinji smiled.

"Because it's lame. And didn't you say you only tease inside the bedroom?"

"So maybe it's both. Which one would you prefer?"

Aki's whole face grew so hot that even the flurries of snow around them couldn't cool him down.

They entered the traditionally styled onsen. Shinji insisted on paying, saying he was always a gentleman on the first date. It got a chuckle out of the old woman who gave them a set of towels and a locker key. Aki followed Shinji down the blue-and-white–titled hallway into the showers and bath.

Aki had expected Shinji to move down a couple of showers once Aki took off his shirt. None of the family members would even shower on the same side at the gym as Aki. Aki understood why. His vitiligo covered his whole body in white patches. It wasn't normal, and being so different wasn't accepted even among yakuza.

But Shinji hadn't moved. In fact, Aki was sure he'd caught Shinji eyeing him a few times. Not that Aki hadn't done the same.

Aki finished washing and stuffed his clothes into the locker above the showers and the briefcase in clear view of the bath. He turned the volume up on his phone and left the locker door open in case Kurosawa called.

Steam rose up from the other side of the large room where

the onsen sat. The hot spring bath was surrounded in stone with wooden accents.

Aki sank into the hot water and leaned his head back against the cool stone. The water loosened his muscles, still tense from the flight and uncomfortable bed. Shinji had the right idea.

Shinji stood before the rocky-edged pool. "You like the view?"

"It's very nice."

"You're not so bad yourself."

Aki shook his head and laughed as Shinji climbed into the water.

"What's so funny?" Shinji asked.

"Let's say it's easier for me to pick up guys in a dark club."

"I think it's kind of hot."

Aki blinked. No one had ever said his skin condition was hot. Even the kids in elementary school had made up a song to make fun of him. Aki had been thankful when he'd gotten into secondary school and could wear pants. Then he could finally put makeup on his face to keep from getting the vacant stares from his classmates.

"Sorry, was I not supposed to say that?" Shinji smiled. "I couldn't help it. Must be the director in me."

Aki could listen to Shinji compliment him all day. It wasn't like Nao ever did.

"You don't have a boyfriend back in Kyoto, do you? Because there might be a fight if you do."

Aki laughed. "Being Father Murata's secretary is a full-time job."

Shinji scooted a little closer. In the clear water, the fact he was half hard was impossible to miss. A wave of desire washed over Aki. Shinji really wanted him that bad? Aki would've doubted it if he hadn't seen it himself.

"What's between you and Murata?" Shinji asked.

"I don't understand what you mean."

"It's impossible to miss how much you're into your boss, but it's clear he doesn't care about you. Maybe you don't have a boyfriend because you don't want to take the time to get one, or you're hoping for something that's not gonna happen," Shinji said.

"I…"

It was like Shinji had slapped him. Had it really been so easy to tell? Aki pressed his lips together. His fantasy of Nao noticing him if he continued to be his devoted servant seemed less likely than noticing a single crane in a thousand-piece chain.

Shinji tilted his head and leaned forward, and Aki was so ready to meet his lips. It had been months since anyone had even gotten close to touching him, and Aki wanted everything Shinji offered. It was stupid to deny himself pleasure when it was so close.

Aki's phone rang, and he pulled back.

"It can wait, can't it?" Shinji said.

Aki was already out of the onsen. "I have to see what Kurosawa wants."

He raced for his phone, his hands dripping water onto his suit.

It was Kohta. Aki's eyes narrowed.

"Hello?" Aki said.

"Where the hell are you? Nao's pissed."

"What happened?"

Aki juggled the phone on his shoulder and pulled on his clothes, not bothering to towel himself off.

"He keeps mentioning how you should be back by now, and then one of the Mafufugumi asked if he wanted tea, and Nao kind of said how there's only one person who can make his tea, and I know it's not me."

Aki pulled on his shirt. It clung to his wet skin, making it hard to button up. "Tell him I'll be there soon."

Shinji sighed and got out of the onsen. "I guess it's time to leave, then."

Aki bowed. "Thank you for helping me today."

Shinji tugged Aki's shirt collar and straightened it. "I would've liked to help you more."

Aki grinned. "Letting me drive back would be helpful."

"Done." Shinji laughed. "Maybe if your boss is nice, he'll let us sit together on the train."

CHAPTER 11

. . .

THE TRAIN CAR to the shitty village in the middle of nowhere was a reject from the forties. The bench seats dug into Nao's thighs, and the advertising hadn't been updated since the war. Not to mention some random kid sat in the corner playing video games with the volume up. All of Nao's thoughts were cut off by electronic-sounding explosions.

Shinji sat across from the Matsukawa trio, which had to be worse than the inconsiderate kid. Every few minutes, Shinji would ogle Aki. Thankfully, Aki knew better than to fall into his trap. Aki completely ignored him, using the briefcase as a table to fold his cranes. He was there to work, not get gawked at by some idiot who made him neglect his duties by taking him to an onsen.

Nao folded his arms.

Sure, maybe Aki had had the right idea getting close to the translator, but because of how few trains ran to the isolated village, they'd be stuck there until the next morning. Watanabe had, yet again, separated Nao from his men by insisting Nao stay the night at Yori's, his mistress's house. It left Kohta and Aki to stay in the Mafufugumi's warehouse. Without Nao there, Aki had no protection from Shinji trying out whatever scandalous thought went through his head.

The train slowed to a stop, and Nao stood. "Let's get this shit show finished."

"It's not like it will get us back home any faster," Kohta mumbled.

Nao glared at him, and he visibly gulped.

"Excuse me, I spoke without thinking," Kohta apologized.

"Take care of the luggage."

Nao left the train right after the little boy, who wandered off into the heavy snow, not looking up from his game. The station was little more than an open wooden structure that seemed more in place to protect the old-fashioned ramen vending machine than to keep out the cold. Snow flurries coated the floor and bench, with more turning the view of everything to a sheet of white.

Aki stepped out of the train, and his eyes grew wide. He held out a hand and approached the vending machine with a smile.

"You hungry?" Nao asked.

Aki shook his head until his hair covered his eyes. Nao wanted to reach out and tuck the stray hairs behind Aki's ear, but he knew better. Aki took in a deep breath, and his lips turned up for a second, then frowned.

"My grandfather used to stock machines like this." If the wind had been any stronger, Nao wouldn't have heard Aki's whisper.

Nao nodded and ran his hand along the bright-yellow siding of the machine. "It looks good considering how many years it's been stuck out here."

"They built them to last. See how the ramen doesn't have a brand listed? It's because each one is made from the vending machine's stocker. So it's like having a personal chef create your meal. Twice a week, our home would be covered in dried noodles as Grandpa put the different spices in each blend."

"We can get some. It'll probably keep us warm in all this cold."

"Sorry." Aki rubbed his eye with his palm and looked away. "You wanted to get the trade over with, not hear me walk down memory lane."

Nao's lips parted. He wanted to say so much more, but nothing came out, as if, even so far away from home, Kyoto had taken his voice for anything more than its service. He walked away, allowing Aki a few moments alone.

Shinji and the group of five other Mafufugumi men he needed for filming left the train.

"We're all ready?" Shinji asked. "No forgotten luggage on the train or anything?"

Nao pushed past Shinji, purposely bumping into his shoulder.

"Hurry up before the snow gets worse." Nao glared.

"Everyone stay close to the person in front of you. It's easy to get lost when it's coming down this hard."

Shinji walked off the platform, and everyone followed in a line behind him. Though the coat warmed his body, Nao's lips and eyes stung from the bitter cold. At points along the hike, Nao couldn't even see farther than the person in front of him.

He glanced back, keeping track of Aki behind him.

Nao let out a heavy sigh, his breath fogging around him. There was no doubt Shinji would try to make a move on Aki during the night. Knowing it aggravated Nao more than if someone had called a taisan drink tea. It couldn't be *tea* unless it was from the plant *Camellia sinensis*. Just like Aki couldn't be Aki unless he was by Nao's side.

Nao rubbed his temple with his gloved hand.

Aki was his own man, and as long as his relationship didn't interfere with his work, Nao shouldn't care.

For the rest of the twenty-minute walk, anytime Nao's thoughts drifted to Aki, he forced himself to remember Miko's bitter words. They'd stung more than the cigarette burn and reminded him to keep focused on the Matsukawa and show her that he could become the leader the Matsukawa needed in her absence.

"It'll be nice and warm inside," Shinji yelled over the whirling snow and pointed to a brown metal warehouse.

He liked to hear himself talk more than Kohta.

The lights on the building reflected the pouring snow. The sidewalk leading to the door cut through the half-meter of snow piled around it.

The wind caught the door, slamming it back into the siding and adding a deeper dent to the one already there. Everything from the thin commercial carpet to the lack of windows in the open space was cheaply retrofitted. There wasn't a single window, and the kitchen cabinets looked like they could be pushed over.

Nao couldn't figure what part was more disgusting: the smell coming from the pot on the hot plate that a Russian was stirring or the Russians themselves. They were seven in total: two by the kitchenette, four playing poker at the dining table, and one napping on the sofa. All of them had tattoos, which was good, since they all had big noses and looked the same.

One of the Russians put down his cards and stood. Tall with blue eyes, he looked like he'd forgotten to shave for a few days. He must've been the leader since he talked first.

He spoke in Russian, and Shinji answered back. Of course, he didn't translate the conversation.

Nao added it to his list of reasons to hate Shinji.

The Russian leader jutted his chin out at Nao then glared at him.

"What does the fucker want?" Nao snapped.

"Nothing." Shinji cleared his throat. "Let's get the exchange started. Mr. Murata, this is Ivan. He's the lea—"

"I don't give a fuck what his name is."

Nao grabbed the briefcase from Aki and tossed it in front of Ivan. His eyes narrowed, but he opened it up nonetheless.

"More now," Ivan spoke in broken Japanese.

"It was five bars, and we brought five," Nao said.

"We wait whole day. Want cash for time."

Nao scoffed. How could Watanabe work with these double-crossing bastards? Well, Watanabe did go back on his agreement with the Matsukawa, so it made sense. Either way, the longer the Russian leader held that smug look on his face, the more Nao wanted to slam his fist into it.

Nao turned to Shinji. "Tell them they'll have better luck

asking to suck my dick than they will asking for more money from us."

It didn't need translating.

One Russian with a bow-tie tattoo on his chest pulled out a knife and approached Nao. Kohta jumped in front of him, but Nao pushed Kohta aside. His help wasn't needed for the slow buffoon.

In a single, quick motion, Nao twisted the Russian's wrist until he dropped the knife. All the adrenaline surged inside. He'd show them what going back on a deal with him meant. Nao snapped up the knife and shoved it in Ivan's stomach.

"There." Nao gave the knife an extra twist and hissed, "Sell your extra kidney if you want the cash."

The Russians' screaming strained Nao's ears. Two of them pulled out guns and aimed them at Nao.

He laughed and approached the one with the knife tattoo on both sides of his neck like someone had stabbed him with it. The Russian muttered something while their leader doubled over and groaned. Shinji stood there shaking, but of course he would; he'd probably never done anything other than direct porn.

Nao smirked at the Russian, who pulled up the barrel of his gun until it was aimed at the center of Nao's forehead.

"If you want to kill me, then do." Nao inched closer, pressing it into his skin.

The Russian's mouth dropped, and the gun shook against Nao's head.

He waited.

Nothing happened.

Without their leader telling them what to do, they were worthless.

"I didn't think so." Nao laughed and stepped away.

Blood seeped out of the wound and covered Ivan's hand. He tried to speak, but nothing came out expect gargled noises. He could take them all out.

"Everyone calm down!" Shinji yelled then said something in Russian.

Shinji and Bow Tie's conversation bounced back and forth, and Nao ignored them, concentrating on the other Russians picking up Ivan and taking him to the bed. Kohta was all smiles, but Aki looked paler than usual. Nao took a step closer to him. It was going to be fine.

Shinji cleared his throat. "They say they'll go ahead with their first agreement."

Nao crossed his arms. "That's what I thought."

"But if Ivan dies before they can leave in the morning, they're going to go after you and your men, Murata."

"If they hadn't changed the agreement in the first place, this wouldn't have happened."

"So you agree to the deal?"

"They can try to go after me, but that means they all have a death wish. Same if they lay a hand on Kohta or Aki."

There was a bit more back-and-forth before they put their weapons away and helped Ivan onto the sofa.

"Okay, everyone agrees," Shinji said then looked toward Nao. "I'll call Yori and tell her you're ready. It's probably a good thing you've got somewhere else to sleep after that."

Shinji went to the far wall to the landline while the Russians grabbed a towel and seemed to debate about what was the best thing to do with the knife.

Nao pulled Aki and Kohta to the other side of the room. The color returned to Aki's face. Hopefully he'd packed enough paper for his cranes to get some sleep during the night. His gentle nature wasn't meant for life in the underworld.

"Watch yourself when you're here," Nao whispered.

Aki nodded.

"If this guy kicks the bucket, you're the first in the line of fire," Nao said. "So don't get too comfortable, and see if you can get the Mafufugumi to give you some weapons, since these guys brought guns."

Kohta grinned. "I'm on it, Boss."

They'd be fine without him. Even Aki could hit the target most of the time when they'd gone shooting.

CHAPTER 12

• • •

AKI SQUINTED AT his phone and turned off the alarm.

Fifteen after four.

Shit.

He'd slept through his first alarm. All the traveling must've taken it out of him. Aki rubbed his eyes.

Who was he kidding? He'd jerked awake at every noise, debating if it had come from Shinji trying to join him in bed or one of the Russians mounting their attack. Maybe Nao had said something to Shinji about not coming in, since it was impossible to misread Shinji's attraction.

Aki slid out of bed and stretched his arms above his head. Thinking Nao cared enough about him to say something to Shinji had to be the biggest lie Aki had told himself in a while. Shinji must've decided he hadn't been worth the hassle.

After a few more stretches and even more self-deprecating thoughts, Aki lay on the thin carpeted floor for his first set of crunches. He'd usually head out to the boxing gym before Nao woke. He still wasn't anywhere near the best fighter, but Hiro, true to his word, taught Aki six days a week. Under his instruction, Aki had gotten better, and Hiro warned him to keep up his workout even while in Hokkaido.

Yet every time Aki counted higher than five, his thoughts drifted back to Shinji.

They'd joked and flirted while the other Mafufugumi members prepared dinner for everyone. Underneath the dining table, Shinji's foot had rubbed up against Aki's, and a few times, his hand had tightly squeezed Aki's. Once Shinji's finger had gingerly brushed over Aki's crotch. But then once dinner was over, Shinji had gotten up and announced he needed to begin filming.

Maybe Aki had missed his chance? Filming might have been Shinji's way of saying "come follow me to the basement." How could Aki be so stupid? Hopefully he hadn't blown his chance.

He stopped mid sit-up and cursed himself for forgetting his place again.

By the time five o'clock rolled around, Aki decided he'd completed his workout even though he couldn't exactly figure out if he'd done all the sets or not.

He showered in the attached bathroom then toweled himself off. He scooped up one of his contacts. Maybe Shinji would be up.

Ouch.

He'd poked himself in the eye.

He groaned, his eye tearing up. The dry weather wasn't helping. Screw it. He rubbed on some foundation and then slipped on his black-framed glasses. He had to get control of himself before he left the room.

He dug through his suitcase and pulled out a stack of origami paper. He began his first crane and quickly followed with a second. Each fold helped him seal away a thought about Shinji until three dozen cranes covered his bed. At least his thoughts were clear even if he'd probably run out of paper on the flight home.

He dressed in full suit and tie then checked his phone. A warning had popped up about bad weather in the area, but the internet signal was too weak to check if the storm had impeded their travel plans. Dialing out proved impossible. Aki groaned. He couldn't do his duty to Nao if he couldn't check up on things. The landline would have to do.

Aki left the room and walked into the hall. Kohta's room was beside his, and the other Mafufugumi members split the other two rooms. Beyond the living area, the other set of bedrooms were Shinji's and the Russians'.

At least there had been some distance between them, but the tension as Aki stepped into the living room was as thick as the night before. Two Mafufugumi didn't seem to mind as they worked on a project on the dining table.

Ivan lay in the same position on the sofa. His comrades were probably too scared to move him with the wound. His body shook as he groped for a blanket just out of reach. He grimaced and let out a groan. The Russian with the bow-tie tattoo on his chest and the other with the split lip listened to the radio, flicking through the static channels before stopping on one playing jazz. They chatted, not attending to their leader at all.

Aki smiled and slowly reached for the blanket. Ivan pulled away and let out a string of Russian between his clenched teeth. Aki froze when the other Russian men stormed over.

"What did you do for that?" Bow Tie yelled at him in broken Japanese.

"He wanted…" Aki shook his head and walked away with his hands up. He didn't need his act of kindness to be interpreted as anything else.

Shinji ran into the room. "What's going on?"

Bow Tie said something and pulled the blanket over Ivan. They spoke to Shinji for a few minutes until he had them laughing.

Aki tried to ignore them, but his gaze kept darting over as he filled the water boiler and set it to the perfect temperature for oolong tea.

"They're a little on edge." Shinji motioned to the Russians, but Aki couldn't take his eyes off Shinji's stomach.

The armholes of his sleeves were cut so low they gave Aki a clear view of his muscular stomach and six-pack abs. Damn. Aki had been training for months and hadn't gotten anywhere near as ripped.

"Wow," Shinji said. "You are cuter with your glasses. The dark frames really suit you."

Aki looked away and tried to not gawk at Shinji's stomach. To make it less obvious, he picked up the landline phone, but there was no dial tone.

Shinji leaned against the counter. "The phones are the first to go during the storm."

"What storm?" Aki asked.

"Don't you hear it?"

The light jazz faded into static. The swirling wind slamming against the metal of the warehouse took Aki's breath away. He'd never heard such a natural, unstoppable force before.

"Blizzards can get scary, but we're safe inside," Shinji said. "We'll be getting a shit ton of snow, though."

Aki's eyes widened. "But the train will still be operational?"

Shinji rubbed the back of his head. "Hard to say. We gotta keep listening to the radio and see."

"Is there a phone I can use? My cell isn't getting any service. I need to call home and tell them we might be longer."

"My phone is nothing but an expensive paperweight here."

"So we have no way to communicate out?"

Shinji squeezed Aki's shoulder. "Don't worry. The tracks will be cleared, and everything will be back in a few days. Think of it as an extra vacation. Though it would've been a lot easier if Murata hadn't stabbed Ivan."

Aki's slapped Shinji's hand away. "Father Murata had every right to do what he did since they went back on their word."

"I'm glad he didn't do it to Watanabe."

Aki's eyes narrowed. Shinji hadn't been at the meeting and couldn't have known Watanabe had gone back on the original agreement. So Watanabe must've planned on forcing the Matsukawa to pay for the whores and told his men before even telling the Matsukawa.

Shinji sighed and lowered his eyes. "Look, I don't have the same relationship with my boss like you and Murata have. Watanabe tells me jack. It might seem like I know more since

I translate, but I'm here to film, and if I don't have the videos up on time, my ass is on the line."

Aki's gaze fell to his feet. His position in the Matsukawa put him at the center of all their plans, so he'd naturally jumped to the conclusion that Shinji would know about Watanabe's plans. But Shinji was a minor cog in the Mafufugumi. He hadn't known anything.

"You drink coffee?" Shinji held out a mug.

Aki took the coffee and drank a few gulps, and Shinji's smile returned. He stepped closer to Aki so that their elbows touched and then rubbed his stomach through the hole of his shirt. Aki's cock stirred. Shinji was such a tease.

"You like the coffee?" he said, his voice low and husky.

"Not when I thought I was going to have it last night."

"I can't tell you how much I wanted to serve you coffee last night." Shinji licked his lips. "I would've gotten you cream and sugar and everything. Believe me, baby, I did, but Watanabe keeps me on a tight schedule. I had to start filming right away."

Aki turned around and looked away from Shinji. "You'll have to make it up to me sometime, then."

"I got time now."

Aki hummed. "Maybe."

"Now who's teasing?"

The dining table was covered in chocolate bonbons. A huge heart-shaped box housed most of them, with a few others half filled.

What's with the chocolate?" Aki asked.

"They're for filming," one of the Mafufugumi answered,

passing off one of the bonbons as he poked a hole into the other.

The other Mafufugumi pushed a syringe into the hole and filled it with a white liquid, then passed it to another, who warmed up the chocolate, smoothed over the hole, and set it in the smaller box.

"Porn is hard," Shinji said.

Aki laughed. "You don't say."

"The lights make it unbearable, and you have to stop and start so much so I can get the best angles. They help keep everyone in the mood. We don't put anything illegal in them. It's the typical stuff they have out at porn sets."

"They really help take the edge off," one of the other Mafufugumi said. "I took two of them and forgot all about what happened during the exchange."

Aki raised a brow. "If it's not illegal, then why are they hiding it in chocolate?"

"Because it tastes better, and I don't have to worry about the marks showing up on camera." Shinji plucked one and held it out to Aki. "Wanna try?"

It wouldn't be the first time Aki had experimented with party drugs. As a teen, he'd once gone to a club, and the guy he'd danced with had told him to stick out his tongue. The bitter taste had stuck with Aki all night, but it had turned out to be some of the kinkiest sex he'd ever had. He'd done it a few times after, but the excitement wore off when one day he'd woken up in a love hotel with five other men he hadn't remembered meeting.

Aki's lips parted, and the scent of chocolate tickled his nose. Images of Shinji tying him to the bed and pounding into him so hard his voice got hoarse vividly flashed through his mind and made his knees tremble. If he reached out and took the chocolate, he'd get to that fantasy sooner rather than later. And the thought of being able to cum multiple times and still have a hard-on turned him on more than it probably should have. Aki licked his lips, but if he took it and Nao walked in, it would be impossible to hide his erection. Probably one look at Nao after eating the chocolate and Aki would've creamed his pants. It was better to wait.

"Maybe later," Aki said. "I need to be ready when Father Murata needs me."

"The storm's still going on, so he's not coming down that mountain anytime soon with the storm raging outside."

"Well, I wanted coffee last night, not this morning." Aki shrugged.

One of the Mafufugumi snickered, but that charming smile crossed Shinji's face. He'd have to work a bit harder to get back on Aki's good side, but if that smile on his face proved anything, it was that he was up for the challenge.

"Guys, that's enough chocolates for now. Why don't we play some cards?"

"I'm up for it."

Without Kohta there, it would promise to be a fair game. Shinji turned to the Russians in the corner and said something to them. They went back and forth for a few minutes before Bow Tie and the one with the split lip pulled up some chairs.

"After a few friendly games, all the bad feelings should be gone," Shinji said. "You and Kohta shouldn't have to live with all this tension just because of what Murata did."

The drugged chocolate was put aside, leaving the untampered bonbons in a heart-shaped box next to a bowl of chips. It might not have been the best breakfast food, but it was better than making something. Shinji passed the cards and popped a chocolate in his mouth.

The first few rounds were stiff, but one of the Russians broke out some cash, and Aki dug into his wallet and pulled some out to join. The split-lipped Russian gave Aki a thumbs-up, and soon everyone had cash on the line.

Sadly, thirty minutes in, Kohta woke up and joined the game as the soft jazz on the radio stopped to announce the train delay.

"That means we're stuck here another day, eh?" Kohta asked.

Shinji glanced over to Ivan. "Unfortunately, yes."

"So we might as well play to keep ourselves sane."

Aki reduced his bets since Kohta's sleight-of-hand card tricks were always on point. Aki had seen him clear out enough tables to know better. But by then, Shinji's foot rubbed up against Aki's leg for a nice distraction.

"So where do you keep the ladies?" Kohta asked.

Shinji pointed to the door beside the kitchenette. "They're down below in the studio."

Kohta nodded and reached over Aki to snatch one of the chocolates.

"You made all the films we saw at the club?"

"Only if you liked them." Shinji laughed. "It's awesome for business. We put it online, and if a girl gets a lot of interest, we sell her to the highest bidder."

Kohta rearranged the cards in his hand. "So who gets to screw them?"

If Kohta wasn't thinking of the latest Versace release, it was how many women he could get wearing it. Aki rolled his eyes and ate one of the chocolates. Bitter dark chocolate was always his favorite. Shinji's hand slipped below the table and squeezed Aki's thigh.

"I see where you're going." Shinji laughed. "I'm up for making you a movie star if you want, but it's not as fun as you think. Lots of stopping and starting, and the lighting gets really hot."

Kohta grinned. "Sounds like a good time."

"Hey! I saw that," Bow Tie yelled in Japanese.

"Saw what?"

The room plummeted into darkness as the power went out in the windowless room. Ivan let out a horrified scream.

CHAPTER 13

• • •

THE FLAME OF Kohta's lighter illuminated the room, followed by the blue glow of phones.

"Power's out," Shinji said. "Happens all the time during a blizzard."

"Is there a backup generator?" Aki asked.

"I'll get some of the other Mafu guys on it. There should be some lanterns here somewhere."

In the warm glow of Kohta's lighter, Bow Tie counted his cash. His eyes narrowed, and he slammed his fist against the table. All the stacked cash toppled over, and Aki flinched.

"You stole!" he shouted.

Kohta wouldn't steal chips. Sure, he might've used his sleight of hand to switch out cards, but he wouldn't turn into an outright thief.

Aki turned on the flashlight feature on his cell phone, casting the table in a beam of white light. "I'm sure we can all come to some kind of—"

Kohta laughed and pushed himself away from the table. "I didn't touch your damn money."

"Give back now."

"I didn't need to steal shit. I had four aces."

Bow Tie clenched his teeth. "Four? Same as last time."

"Just because you're—"

The Russian launched himself at Kohta, knocking them both to the ground. The table flipped over, causing the money to flutter around the room. The veins in Bow Tie's neck popped out as he grabbed Kohta's collar. Kohta held up his arms to cover his face.

Aki backed away.

Kohta had gotten himself into the mess, but it would look bad on both him and Nao if something happened. Shinji ran between them, putting a hand on the Russian's powerful arm. He said something in Russian and got a bunch of angry shouts in return. Yet Shinji stayed calm and kept his voice low.

Then slowly, Bow Tie's grip loosened until Kohta's shirt slid out of his hands.

"Are you crazy?" Aki groaned.

"I wasn't cheating. I swear."

"You knew exactly what you were doing."

Kohta's reply was a sly grin as he brushed back his hair as blood dripped from his lip. He could be such a selfish prick sometimes. Aki rubbed his forehead, cleaning away a thin layer of sweat. All the commotion was making his whole body hot.

"You're making this harder on all of us," Aki said. "The storm covered the tracks, and who knows how long we're trapped here.

It's better if we make friends so we don't get killed in our sleep."

"Fine." Kohta crossed his arms. "Shinji, you can tell him to keep all the damn money if he wants. I'll win it all back anyway."

Shinji translated, and the Russian smiled, picking up the strewn cash.

"So everyone's good?" Aki asked.

"As long as Kohta doesn't win too many games next time," Shinji replied.

Aki closed his eyes and shook his head. Kohta strolled back to his bedroom as if nothing had happened. At least that was one less thing to worry about.

One of the Mafufugumi members clicked on a lantern and then another, spreading a few others around the room.

Aki swallowed, but an uncontrollable heat rolled over him. He grabbed on to the nearest chair to steady himself. It must have been all the excitement getting to him.

Shinji turned up the table. "You feeling all right?"

"I'm fine." It was a bigger lie than Kohta saying he hadn't cheated.

"I'll see what's taking it so long to turn on."

Shinji disappeared, and a wave of heat punched Aki. He put his arm on the table and buried his head on it. His skin prickled. He loosened his tie and unbuttoned the first few buttons of his shirt.

He'd be worthless to Nao if he'd come down with a cold. Maybe they had a sports drink in the fridge. Then he could stop the cold before it started.

He stood, but the room spun, and all the blood from his

head drained into the least convenient place. He stumbled back in his chair. The next button of his shirt came undone, and he rubbed his neck and collarbone. His other hand slipped to his inner thigh, then up.

Aki's body shook. He couldn't stop touching himself. It was the only way to get some relief from the heat burning inside him. It wasn't so much heat radiating out of his skin but more his cock pulsing the heat throughout his whole body. Aki moaned and pressed his hand against it.

He needed release, and even going to the bathroom would delay it too much.

"The generator got snowed in," Shinji said, coming back into the room. "They're digging it out now."

Aki tried to look up, but the room spun again. He buried his head in the crook of his arm. His other hand, however, couldn't leave the intense wanting need in his dick. He rubbed himself through the rough fabric of his pants. Waves of pleasure washed through him, more intense than ever before.

He moaned, fogging up his glasses. He was going to explode right there, but nothing he did was enough to push him over the edge. He knew he should've been embarrassed, but the exhibitionist aspect only made it hotter.

Aki grasped his belt buckle—

Shinji put his hand on Aki's shoulder, and the other's touch brought a glint of satisfaction.

He needed Shinji.

He needed his hands all over him.

He needed to be inside of him or for Shinji to shove his dick so far up him it tickled Aki's throat.

It didn't matter what, as long as it brought him to his peak.

"You don't look so good." Shinji leaned down, his breath caressing Aki's ear. "Why don't we head back to my bedroom."

Shinji offered his hand to Aki, who grabbed it, then stumbled to lean on his shoulder. As they made their way to the back, Shinji's voice grew more alluring with each word he spoke, even though Aki was too drunk with lust to bother comprehending it all.

The bedroom was sparse, considering the amount of time Shinji said he spent in the warehouse. A double bed sat in the center with a mountain of blankets strewn about. With a gentle nudge, Aki plopped onto the bed.

The lights clicked on.

Shinji shrugged. "They must've dug out the generator."

"Shinji, I…" Aki whispered then looked at the bulge in his pants.

A soft glow formed around Shinji. "It's okay. I know what you need."

Shinji leaned forward, one hand wrapping around Aki's hand and his other palm holding Aki's cheek. Aki nuzzled into it like a cat. He needed more, and he'd had enough of Shinji's teasing. Aki wiggled his hands out of Shinji's grip and moved it from his thigh to his crotch.

"This is what I need," Aki said.

"Oh, is it?"

Electricity shot through Aki as Shinji traced the outline of his cock. Aki had never felt so turned on in his life. Though, he'd never been with someone so hot before. Aki opened his legs wider, silently begging for more, but Shinji's touch was feather light.

"Now." Aki leaned back.

The room tilted, but Aki closed his eyes and focused on Shinji's hand. Each little nudge and massage through the fabric of his pants sent Aki's toes curling. Aki swallowed back a moan, feeling closer to climax than ever before but never reaching it.

He opened himself up wider, hoping the angle would change it, but no matter how hard Shinji seemed to press, it only left Aki more frustrated.

"I have to confess I've been attracted to you from the moment I saw you," Shinji said.

"Then fuck me."

"I see how you play it. You act all innocent and collective with that elegant Kyoto dialect, but you really want it hard like the whores I film."

The pure wanting desire, the forwardness of it all. But everything was so hot, and each pump of blood throughout his body begged for more.

"So what of it?"

Shinji chuckled. "Is that what you want then? For me to fuck you like a whore?"

"Yes."

Then Shinji's hand was gone. Aki groaned, but then Shinji's finger drew little circles on Aki's hand.

Aki groaned. "What are you doing?"

"Your hands are really pretty," Shinji said.

"I don't want you to play with my hands."

"Oh, I know."

Shinji nipped at Aki's neck and then kissed him. First Shinji's tongue swept over Aki's lips as if tasting to see if he was good enough to dive inside. Aki opened his mouth, and Shinji entered, his tongue caressing over Aki, leaving a lingering salt taste Aki's body craved more of.

Shinji slipped out of Aki's mouth and kissed his collarbones. He popped free the next button of Aki's shirt, kissing the newly exposed skin. Each kiss left Aki's skin burning. Shinji traced each of the white stretches of skin across Aki's chest.

He'd never had anyone pay so much attention to his imperfections. So many would've turned off the lights already, but Shinji hadn't even suggested it.

Shinji dipped his tongue in Aki's belly button. Aki gasped and clutched onto Shinji's arm. Everything was going slower than Aki wanted. Each minute of Shinji's utmost attentiveness sent a wave of heat through Aki he'd never experienced before.

Shinji folded his arms on Aki's thighs and rubbed his finger underneath the hem of his pants.

"It's so beautiful," Shinji said.

Aki grabbed Shinji's wrist and pushed it down his pants as far as the buckle of his belt would allow. "Stop teasing me already."

Shinji tugged at the line of hair Aki guided him to while his other hand traced the patch of uncolored skin by his nipple.

"Is down here like up here?" he asked.

Aki moaned, bringing his legs up, but Shinji's strong arms pushed them down.

"You're so hot," Shinji said.

Aki groaned. "Then do me hard."

"If that's the way you like it—but I want to remember each moment of this." Shinji unzipped Aki's pants and pulled out his cock. "I mean, look at it—it's wonderful. I love the little band of white here and down here."

Shinji's tongue traced around Aki's head and then lower around his base. Then he twirled it around the tip, collecting the precum there. Out of desperation for more of his mouth, Aki bucked his hips up. He hit the sweet heat of the back of Shinji's throat, but Shinji gagged and pulled away.

Shinji grabbed one of Aki's hands and wrapped it around Aki's own stiff member. "Can you take over from here? Just like you were going to do out in front of everyone. It was so damn sexy."

Aki threw his head back and moaned, his hand working on his cock. Through half-lidded eyes, he saw Shinji rub himself and then grab a camera he had on the nightstand.

"Damn, baby, it's so fucking hot." He held up the camera. "This is okay, yeah? I can't get enough of it."

Shinji could've asked if it was okay for everyone in the house to watch and Aki would've agreed.

CHAPTER 14

· · ·

NAO CLUTCHED HIS fingers together and stared at the burn mark, now puss filled and white. He could be the blood-thirsty demon Miko wanted him to be, but he could learn how to be more than that.

The howl of the wind hung like the silence before the storm.

The Koreans would attack.

Kyoto needed him there.

And he was stuck in the shit village for another day.

Nao shook his head and continued his descent to the ware-house. Since he'd stepped foot on Hokkaido, all of Nao's nights had turned into sleepless tossing and turning, like every cell in his body screamed for him to head back home. Regardless of the burn on his wrist, he was a good leader, but being away from Kyoto at such a crucial time made him look bad in front of his men.

"Fuck," Nao groaned as his leg sank into the snow.

He broke free and continued down to the Mafufugumi

warehouse. Nao pulled opened the door, but the wind caught it and it banged against the metal building. Gritting his teeth, he grasped the end and slammed it shut behind him.

Aki wasn't in the living room.

Shinji wasn't either.

Were they together?

Nao bit his cheek. He shouldn't care. It was safer for everyone if he didn't.

Ivan still lay on the sofa,, getting spoon-fed by a Russian with a split lip. He must've had it sliced in two and it hadn't healed back evenly. Everything would've been so much easier for them if they'd stuck with the original deal.

Kohta played cards with three Mafufugumi at the other side of the room. They'd lose their shirts if Kohta wanted. But seeing how the cash flow looked, Kohta wasn't really trying.

Nao approached the game. They all stood and bowed.

"We had some chili for lunch. I can reheat some for you," Kohta said.

"Yori made sure she kept me fed," Nao said.

Somehow between taking care of a pack of five dogs and a horde of children, she'd made a traditional butadon for him. The sweet and savory gravy on the savory pork was so mouthwatering he'd almost forgotten the baby screaming in his ear. Watanabe must've told her what Nao liked before he'd arrived.

"I'll make you some tea, then," one of the Mafufugumi offered.

Nao chuckled. "I don't think so. Only Aki makes my tea. Where is he?"

Kohta winked. "Shinji's been taking good care of him the past few hours."

Hours?

All the muscles inside Nao tensed. His jaw locked tight. It was exactly like he'd predicted. Aki should've known better than to go off with some reject yakuza.

Nao swallowed. "That's good for him. Where do they have you sleeping, Kohta?"

"Back there." Kohta cocked his head to one of the hallways.

He was never one to pick up on subtle hints, or maybe he didn't want to leave the game. Either way, what Kohta lacked in perception he made up for in his accuracy with a gun, which was really all he needed in a bodyguard.

"Why don't you show me," Nao said.

"Oh." Kohta tossed his cards on the table. "You guys are lucky."

Kohta grabbed the stack of cash in front of him to the relief of the Mafufugumi players. Kohta took Nao down a hallway and into a small room with a single bed.

"If you're here, where's Aki's room?" Nao's thoughts slipped out of his mouth without thinking.

"I think next door. I know Shinji's on the other side of the warehouse."

Nao cleared his throat. "Good. It'll spread out the Russians if they attack. Have you noticed anything suspicious while you were here?"

"The Mafu guys suck at poker. I don't even have to use any tricks to win."

Nao crossed his arms. Aki was so much better at knowing what he needed. Aki should've realized he was there by now. Nao sighed. It was one thing to have a little side romance, but if it was going to interfere with Aki's duties, he'd have to forbid it.

A small grin crossed his face.

"What's got you so happy all of a sudden?" Kohta asked. "It's not like we played strip poker."

"It's more that you'd think I would care about the gambling skills of our supposed allies."

Kohta shrugged. "I found it odd. I also asked some of the guys if they had any weapons we could have, but they said they had none."

"That is suspicious."

"I think they only work on Shinji's films and back at the brothel. They're not like real yakuza. They said they'd never worked on the streets or anything."

"Just like Watanabe not to give all his men formal training."

"Not like you, huh? You had me on my knees for months." Kohta sat on the bed and ran his finger along his lush lips. "Boss, I wanted to ask you something."

Kohta's blond hair dropped over half his face. Nao bit the inside of his cheek. Kohta knew how to take advantage of his looks. A few months prior and it would've been a different story. Aki hadn't dared mention Nao's lax disciplinary treatment of Kohta, but there had been times when after a certain request from Kohta, he'd caught the sour expression on Aki's face.

Nao groaned. "What do you want?"

"Shinji said I could be in one of the movies. Can I do it?"

"You want to be a porn star all of a sudden?"

"You think I could really become a star?"

Nao rubbed his temple. They weren't really having this conversation, were they?

"Please, Boss."

"I don't know."

Kohta tilted his head. "There was something else I noticed. The Russian with the bow tie tattoo seems to be the new leader. His temper lasted as long as me resisting a Louis Vuitton sale."

"Were you holding on to that in case I didn't say yes right away?"

"I would've told you eventually."

Nao sighed. "As long as it doesn't get in the way of your job, it's fine."

There was a knock on the door, then a faint sound of Aki's voice.

"Come in," Nao ordered.

Aki gave a formal bow. "Excuse my—"

"What took you so long?"

Aki kept his gaze lowered. His hair looked knotted like it hadn't been brushed all day. His dark framed glasses only magnified his large almond-colored eyes. What was he doing wearing them during working hours?

"I humbly beg your forgiveness," Aki said. "I think, perhaps, I'm coming down with a cold."

Hopefully that was all he'd caught from Shinji.

Nao took a step forward. "Your main concern should be serving me and the family."

"Absolutely. My thoughts and actions are always to bring you pleasure."

"I'm finding it harder to believe since we've arrived in Hokkaido." The words sounded too harsh to Nao's ears, but he couldn't take them back. He couldn't appear weak.

Aki pressed his lips together and slowly nodded.

"Tell me. What have you done for the family lately?" Nao pushed.

"Please excuse my lack of progress, but the phone isn't getting reception here, and the landline is down."

"So you've done nothing."

Aki's mouth fell open, and Nao glared at him. There was nothing Aki could say to get out of it. Nao took in a deep breath and waited. He had all the time in the world and wasn't going to bend.

After a few seconds, Aki managed to squeak out, "Please—"

Nao brushed past Aki. "It's clear that if I need anything done on this trip, I'll have to do it myself. Where is Shinji? I want some answers."

Kohta shot up. "If he's not with Aki, then he's probably filming below."

Nao forged ahead through the hallway and into the studio. Aki's feet dragged along the threadbare carpet behind Nao, who suppressed the urge to look back. Aki's job was too important for him to be distracted. The Koreans could've attacked, and Kurosawa could have called a hundred times asking for orders, but there was no way to know.

Aki clutched onto the wall as they stepped on the creaking stairs to the lower level.

All the money for the warehouse had gone to Shinji's film studio. Studio lights lined the ceiling, and three fabricated sets showed different-styled bedrooms scattered around the area. Two stationary cameras were on either side of the set, while Shinji held on to a hand-held camera. Underneath all the prestige, the underlying scent of burnt hair was inescapable.

One of the Mafufugumi members was there with one of the ladies. She looked a little out of it but met the guy's thrusts and looked like she was enjoying it.

"Now hold still so I can get a close-up," Shinji directed.

Nao cleared his throat.

Shinji lowered the camera. "Mr. Murata."

"Where are the women the Matsukawa bought?"

"I'm kind of in the middle of filming."

"I don't care."

Shinji's knuckles turned white as he grasped the camera. "I need to upload videos every day, or else the profits drop."

"Then Kohta can film."

"I don't think—"

Nao closed the space between him and picked off a piece of lint from Shinji's shirt then patted his shoulder before squeezing it into a vise grip.

"Are you really going to tell me no?" Nao asked.

Shinji gulped. "Of course not.

"I didn't think so."

Shinji's hands shook as he handed Kohta the camera. What had Aki seen in such a pathetic creature?

Kohta licked his lips and went over to the action. Nao caught a glimpse of Aki lifting his gaze to meet Shinji's. Yet in Aki's eyes wasn't lust but anger.

Nao smiled to himself.

"What's with the smell?" Nao asked.

Shinji laughed. "That was when I tried to do something more visual with a dungeon set, but one of the candles got knocked over. You can still see some of the scorch marks. Luckily, we keep the different sets on hand, so it was easy to replace and didn't slow down filming."

Scorch marks scraped the wall above one of the sets. They almost reached the ceiling, so it had to have been a big fire.

"What else can I do for you?" Shinji asked.

"How many ladies did the five bars of gold buy?"

"About twenty."

"About?"

Shinji rubbed his neck. "Seventeen to be exact."

"Doesn't seem like a fair price at all."

"I mean—I ah, sometimes they give us more. It varies."

"The women must know the location of Yamashita's treasure if they're worth that much. I want to see them."

"We keep them this way."

Shinji escorted them past the open filming set down a hallway. The only door had a newly replaced lock from the way the paint job looked. Shinji unlocked the door and opened it.

Nao glanced inside. All the young women inside looked in

their late teens and twenties. They all lounged around looking a little sleepy, but nothing out of the ordinary. Something about it wasn't adding up. Five bars for a little over a dozen was outrageous. Maybe Shinji had some agreement with the Russians, and he'd skimmed some off the top.

"You have enough food for them since the storm has us all stuck here for who knows how long?" Nao asked.

"I usually spend a few weeks filming them, and when I leave, Yori restocks enough food for everyone. Sometimes she even comes by to teach the women some Japanese phrases."

"I see."

"Anything else?" Shinji asked.

"That's all for now."

Shinji locked the door then ran back to get the camera from Kohta, but Nao stayed put. Aki hadn't looked up from his shoes, and his fingers twitched as if begging for pieces of paper to calm his nerves. Nao could order him to speak and get whatever he was thinking out in the open to kill the sullen mood he was in. But whatever emotions Aki was dealing with were his. He'd put himself in that position, and it wasn't Nao's place to dig them out.

Nao called Kohta over.

Kohta grinned. "Do you think if I ask, Shinji will give me a directing credit?"

"Will you be serious for even five minutes?" Nao snapped.

"Sorry, it's just with all the tension with the Russians, I've got to do something to get my mind off it."

"Then actually do your job and set up a plan if the Russians attack." Nao turned toward Aki. "You said you couldn't get a message out at all?"

Aki shook his head. "It was impossible to even get a signal."

"Clearly Shinji has the internet since he's uploading videos. Make him show you so we can get some communication established with home. Got it?"

"I won't fail you."

Nao caught a glimpse of the burn on his wrist and tugged on his jacket sleeve.

"Remember, if you see anything, tell me right away. With the landline down, you'll have to climb up the mountain to get to me."

"Okay, Boss," Kohta said, while Aki nodded.

"I could use some tea. You feeling well enough to make some?"

Aki smiled. "Anything you desire, Father Murata, I will fulfill."

There was the Aki Nao knew. They headed back upstairs with Nao leading the way and Aki behind him. Nao turned the handle to open the door, and there stood one of the Russians. His shirt was open, revealing a bow tie tattoo.

Bow Tie then spat in Aki's face. "Fucking homo."

CHAPTER 15
• • •

AKI WINCED AND wiped the spit off his face.

Nao growled and jumped on the Russian. They toppled down the stairs, knocking Kohta and Aki down. Aki tried to brace himself, but the air was knocked out of him during the fall.

There was no escaping the distinct crunch when Nao raised his fist and smashed it against the Russian's face. His blood spattered centimeters away from Aki. He squinted, and the world blurred since his glasses flew off in the assault.

"Let's fuck him up!" Kohta yelled, jumping into the fight.

Nao's fist blurred as it pounded on the Russian's face, while Kohta held him down for Nao to keep up his assault. Aki found his glasses and slipped them on. A tingling spread through his limbs. Nao was going all out for him. Just the sheer power behind each swing took Aki's breath away.

Shinji's voice rang out in a slur of Japanese and Russian. He pushed Kohta aside and tugged the Russian out of Nao's grip. Of course, Nao didn't have a scratch on him. Kohta's shirt had been ripped in the struggle, but the only blood came from the Russian's nose and mouth.

Nao straightened his tie and looked at Aki. "You okay?"

Aki smiled. Shinji helped the Russian up, who said something, then spat out some blood.

"What did he say?" Nao asked.

"He was apologizing," Shinji said.

Aki didn't need to understand Russian to know that wasn't an apology. The sour Russian used his shirt to plug his nose and wandered toward the back studio.

Nao crossed his arms. "We should kill them all off and be done with the tension. Then get our gold back."

Shinji cleared his throat. "Watanabe wouldn't want an undue burden with the Russians."

"Believe me, it wouldn't be undue. They all deserve their nose broken and more."

Nao turned and headed up the stairs as Shinji called for a break in filming.

Aki followed behind Nao, and once they reached the top of the stairs, the rest of the Mafufugumi greeted them. They blocked the door from the line of Russians behind them. The looks on their faces could kill.

Nao pushed past them and pulled Aki and Kohta outside. The cold breeze sent a shiver down Aki's spine, but it was the best way to deescalate the situation. Nao's forehead wrinkled, and his breath came out of his nose like a dragon.

Aki pressed his lips together as Nao paced. Kohta might've done a bit much defending Aki like that, but Aki's heart had sunk with each punch Nao had delivered.

"No matter how much I want to slit those Russians' throats, our hands are tied until they make the first move," Nao said.

Kohta hit his fist into his open palm. "Too bad Shinji cut in. I was ready to show that bow-tie asshole a piece of my mind. He can't talk about Aki that way."

"If the asshole does it again, you break his nose for a second time." Nao shook his head and pointed to a peak on the hill above. "It's about a twenty-minute walk, but I'm straight up there if you need me. I don't think I can stay much longer without killing one of those bastards."

Kohta cracked a smile. "It wouldn't be much of a loss."

"Too bad Watanabe needs these bastards so much." Nao laughed and gave Kohta a playful punch on the shoulder. "Don't get too distracted by your dick that you forget to see what's in front of you."

Kohta gave him a thumbs-up. "Sure, Boss."

"Aki, I need a connection back home. If the Koreans attack while we're stuck, it will be a nightmare, so it's important to get that line back home."

Aki's stomach tightened. He could tell him how the Koreans had already attacked a historic site like they'd done during their last turf war.

"I won't fail you," Aki said.

"Good."

Nao smiled and stretched his hand out like he was going to squeeze Aki's shoulder, but he stopped and pulled it away. Aki's heart sank. Even with everything, Nao still wouldn't even touch him. He had to give up hoping. After all, he'd already slept with Shinji. Aki's face grew warm. It was mostly the stupid drug he'd accidently eaten that had done it though. He should've realized after that first bite and jacked off in the bedroom alone.

Maybe the whole trip to Hokkaido was fate's way of showing him he needed to move on. Maybe Shinji was really the right choice.

Nao walked off, and Aki clenched his fist. He wouldn't fail Nao again. Aki turned to head back inside, but the huge grin on Kohta's dumb face stopped him.

Aki crossed his arms. "What's that about?"

"It was nice to see you going after someone who isn't the boss."

"You could show some more respect by using his proper title."

"What? You and Shinji are a good thing."

"Calling our godfather 'Boss' leaves a bad impression for everyone around."

"Don't change the subject. You and Shinji are a good thing. I've been trying to get you over Boss since the fall season of Versace was released."

Aki crossed his arms. "You want Shinji to like me so he'll ask you to be in more films."

"I've been trying to get you to meet tons of guys. Figured you'd be less grumpy if you were getting laid, and I was right. You've been pleasant since you met Shinji. This morning you were downright chipper."

Aki rolled his eyes and opened the door. "I've got work to do. You should, too."

"Just so you know, you're totally loud. I think I heard you moaning from my bedroom."

The heat rushed through to Aki's face worse than if he'd stuck his face in the water boiler.

Kohta laughed. "You should see your face. I was joking."

"It wasn't funny."

He stepped inside and straight into his bedroom. He showered and changed into the freshest suit he'd packed. Even with the cold drying out his eyes, he poked in his contacts. The last thing he wanted was for Shinji to think he wasn't working.

Shinji stood by the microwave as a bowl of leftover chili heated. He spoke in Russian to the three gathered around. Aki walked over, and the Russians scattered.

"Let's go somewhere more quiet," Aki said.

Shinji grinned. "Your bedroom or mine?"

Aki dug his fingernails into his palm. "Yours."

The internet connection was probably set up in Shinji's room. Even if Aki wasn't ashamed of what he and Shinji had done, the fact it all blurred into a fog made Aki's stomach twist. He'd at least wanted to remember the details of the sex.

Shinji took his bowl and spooned the chili into his mouth as he meandered to his bedroom. He opened the door and took a few more bites before putting the bowl on the nightstand.

He opened his mouth, but Aki spoke before he could get a word in. "Why didn't you tell me you had the internet? I need to contact home."

"You never said you needed it."

"Well, I do."

Shinji shrugged. "Then use it, but it's super slow. Uploading videos is a twenty-four-hour kind of thing here. So it probably won't work."

"I need to do this now."

Shinji pulled out a laptop from underneath the bed, a blue ethernet cable sticking out of the side. Aki climbed onto the bed and clicked on a new internet tab.

Shinji trailed a hand down Aki's arm, sending little pulses of excitement through him. Even if he couldn't remember their time together, his body sure did, and in a way even that excited Aki.

"Sorry, babe." Shinji said. "I never knew you wanted it. It must be hard to work for Murata."

The swirling circle on the page stopped and loaded an error page. Aki groaned.

"Can't you pause the video upload?" Aki asked.

"Sorry, it's pretty much automatic. And Watanabe needs those videos uploaded every day. You understand—you gotta do what the boss wants."

Aki rubbed his temple. "So, when this one is done, I can hop on to send a few emails?"

"Remember, I said they were automatic. I got all the videos set for the day."

Aki lay back and gazed at the stained drop-down ceiling. He'd disappointed Nao once already; he wasn't going to let it happen again. Even if it was probably time to give up on wishing for a romance between them, Aki still respected Nao.

Shinji was being unreasonable in not allowing Aki to pause

the videos to check that Kyoto wasn't set ablaze and under the thumb of the Korean mob overlord.

Aki sighed. He'd been out of it since he'd woken up, and a splitting headache had taken root in the center of his forehead. No—it was after he'd played poker with everyone. Then he'd hooked up with Shinji, but it was more of a blur than the night Aki had been finally old enough to get into his first gay bar.

"About this morning." Aki stroked Shinji's muscled arm.

"It was nice, wasn't it?"

"I hadn't meant to take one of those drugged chocolates."

"What? We were all eating the chocolate. One of the guys must have forgotten to put it in the done pile."

Aki shook his head, letting his hair fall into his eyes. "I can't believe I jacked off in front of you like that. We don't really know each other, and—"

"Why were you embarrassed?"

"I just told myself I would stop randomly hooking up with people after I joined the yakuza."

Shinji smiled. "That's easy, then, because I'm still right here, and what you did was freaking hot, and it's not like Murata cares what you do in your downtime. He's not the boss of your sex life."

"And I even let you record it."

"It was the hottest thing I've filmed in a long time."

"That's why I stopped taking them. I always did the most embarrassing shit trying to fit in. So delete the video."

"It's not like I'm going to do anything. It's in my private collection."

"I don't want it out there."

Shinji turned over. "Why, do you not trust me?"

Aki pressed his lips together.

"So now you're going to treat me like Murata does and not trust a damn word I say? Do you know how hard it is to keep the Russians from turning on you guys right now?"

"I…"

"Even if everything turns out okay, they're going to tell Watanabe what happened. My head's the one that's going to roll for all of this. It's so much pressure." He sighed and looked at Aki. "And here I thought we had something special, Aki. I thought you were able to really relax and be yourself around me, and now I see I was wrong about that. You think I'm doing something behind your back."

Aki bit his lip. "I don't think that."

Shinji wrapped Aki in a hug and kissed him. Aki's toes curled, and he deepened the kiss. Aki's tongue dove inside Shinji's mouth, taking full dominance over him.

"I'm sorry," Aki said. "I shouldn't have overreacted like that."

"That's okay. Will you kiss me like that again?"

Aki smirked. "I'm going to do a lot more than that. Prepare for your world to be rocked."

By the time Aki was done with him, Shinji would be sleeping it off too soundly to even notice Aki pausing the video upload to contact home.

CHAPTER 16

•••

"DOES YOUR PHONE work?" Nao asked, plucking a scrap of meat between the bones of his grilled mackerel.

Yori laughed. "Those are the first thing that goes out during a storm."

"Was that you this morning chopping wood, then? What's with the huge wood pile outside for anyway?"

"It's for the fireplace."

"There's a fireplace?"

"In the master bedroom." She gave a peaceful sigh and spoon-fed one of her children in the high chair beside her. "Watanabe might not seem it, but he's very romantic."

With four children and a fifth on the way, it was like Watanabe had decided to raise the birthrate of Japan all by himself. Nao couldn't see what was romantic about Watanabe abandoning

Yori in the middle of nowhere to raise a horde of children by herself. The poor woman's hair looked like it hadn't been cut since she'd had her oldest, Giichi, their seven-year-old son.

"He let me design this whole house," she continued. "I used to watch tons of those black-and-white Hollywood romance movies. Mae West is my favorite actress, and in one movie, she had a fireplace in the bedroom. Since then, I always dreamed of having one, and Watanabe gave me that."

The whole house looked slightly dated; perhaps Yori's old Hollywood style was the cause of it, or the fact she was a mistress and not a wife. For the number of children Yori had, the three-bedroom house was cramped. Nao had been given the oldest child's, Giichi's room, while the day Nao stayed at Watanabe's wife's home, he'd had a room to himself. She even only had two children.

Many yakuza had mistresses, so it wasn't uncommon for them to have one or more women on the side with a string of illegitimate children. Nao was lucky his father had loved his mom so much he never had taken any mistresses. Nao's hand clenched into a fist. Even when his mom left, his father had kept to himself. He probably hadn't wanted another disappointment of a child.

"Sorry, did you mean to say my chopping wood this morning woke you up?" Yori asked. "I'm surrounded by children all day. They're not as tactful when it comes to something they don't like."

She had chopped right outside the window, and what yakuza wouldn't wake up at the sound of an ax?

"You have enough to last you three winters."

Yori laughed. "I know. It's more of a stress relief than anything. The kids can play outside, and I just start chopping."

Nao nodded, eating another piece of fish. Giichi mimicked Nao, picking at his mackerel. The two young girls, five and four, had a diet of hot dogs cut to resemble octopus. Yori had explained during lunch they refused to eat anything else. One of them wasn't even eating the hot dog, instead building a small cabin out of a log toy and shoving her little baby doll inside.

Nao set his chopsticks across his plate, and Giichi mirrored him. Nao gave a half smile. It was kind of cute.

"How many times do I have to say don't feed the dogs!" Yori scolded and shooed the small dog away, then picked up a half-eaten octopus hot dog off the floor.

Yori had almost as many dogs as children. Maybe they came together as a pair. The birth of one meant another dog joined the pack as well. One was as big as a miniature pony the younger kids could ride around on. The smallest was a kickable rat. Their barking and the sound of nails against the wooden floors had kept Nao up half the night. Nao shook his head. He missed the quiet company of his cat the longer he stayed in the busy house.

"Giichi, help Mommy with the dishes," Yori said.

"But Mom—"

"Now."

Giichi slid off the chair and smiled at Nao. "Are you finished, Mr. Murata?"

Nao pushed the plate toward Giichi, and he cleared the rest of the table while Yori cleaned off the kid in the high chair. Nao's mom had always made him help with the dishes and tried to keep Nao distracted by filling up his time with elementary cram school. She'd point out how he needed to study hard because his education was the only thing no one could take from him. Nao had suspected it was more to keep him from falling into the family businesses. In the end, it hadn't helped, and she'd abandoned him after he screwed up.

"Have you thought of starting your own family?" Yori asked.

Nao stood. One of the larger dogs sniffed the ground for any crumbs. The two girls abandoned their place at the table and danced into the living room then rummaged through a toy bin.

"Children would be impossible," Nao said.

"I know about the whole gay thing." Yori smiled. "That's the only reason Watanabe allowed you to stay with me. He gets pretty jealous. He doesn't even allow me to go down to the safe house. Worried all the guys will start getting ideas."

Nao crossed his arms. Shinji had said that Yori would go down there and teach the ladies Japanese phrases. It must've been another lie.

"But you know—" Yori hitched up the kid on her hip. "—Even just one son to carry on the family name?"

"Like a sham marriage?"

"Plenty of men do it."

"The thought never crossed my mind."

"It must be different for men, then. I always wanted children." She shook her head. "What does your family think?"

"They're all dead."

"Seems more of a reason to have them if you ask me."

Giichi looked up at Nao. "You want to play Mario?"

Nao snorted. He hadn't even played Mario as a kid. It wasn't like they'd been allowed video games at the detention center,

and when he got out, his dad had stuck him in the care of Nakamura. Nakamura had hated technology and had broken the
Game Boy Nao had tried to hide. Nakamura had given him
such a beating he hadn't touched anything remotely advanced
until he'd gotten his own apartment.

"Giichi, leave Mr. Murata alone," Yori said. "And just because
school is canceled doesn't mean you can play. You should be
studying."

Giichi ignored her, opening a cabinet underneath the TV
in the living room and pulling out his games to show Nao. He
talked about the different types, but Nao only half listened,
taking in the house. It had been the height of style ten years ago.
Even Giichi's game system appeared beat up and overused. If
Watanabe was so romantic, why wouldn't he shower Yori with
the latest of everything? So many yakuza wives and mistresses
were bathing in luxury; it was like Yori was forgotten.

Giichi shoved a controller into Nao's hand, and the next
thing he knew, he was in control of Princess Peach in some
tropical water park.

A bit of nostalgia bubbled up in Nao for the times he'd play
his own Mario game at home with his dad while his mother
cheered them on.

He glared at his wrist. His father wouldn't have played games
with him if he'd known how much of a disappointment his son
would grow up to be. The Murata line would die with him, and
he'd become a yakuza, the last thing both of his parents had
wanted.

"Watch out!" Giichi yelled. "You're going to get killed if you
stand there like that. You've got to jump."

Nao mumbled an apology and followed Giichi's orders.

They played for a few minutes. Giichi was nice about Nao's utter failure, but all the advice the kid gave about what buttons to press was lost on Nao.

Giichi helped them clear a few levels before his mom came in and turned off the TV.

"Mom! We were at the boss."

"It's time for a walk."

She wore a large coat that doubled the size of her pregnant belly. The horde of dogs whined at the door, and the smaller children were all wrapped up in bright-colored puffy coats. Their limbs looked so small they appeared like little mounds of mochi.

"We never used to go for walks," Giichi groaned.

"Let's give Mr. Murata some peace."

Giichi took the remote controller from Nao, wrapped it up, and put it in its rightful place.

"We can defeat the boss after the walk."

Nao chuckled. "Sure."

"Now go get on your coat, Giichi," Yori said.

He walked out of the room and to his bedroom that Yori had set up as the guest room. The poor kid had to share a room with his younger sisters.

"Sorry he keeps bugging you. He misses his father."

Nao shrugged. "Does Watanabe only visit you just to give him another kid?

"It sure seems that way." She rubbed her belly and laughed. "When he does, he stays for a few days and then goes back to the city."

Giichi came out in a puffy green jacket and opened the door. "Come on, Mom. The sooner we leave, the sooner we get back."

All the dogs ran out, barking at their newfound freedom. Yori sighed and grabbed the hands of the little girls.

The door shut behind them, and Nao lay on the sofa, getting the moment of silence he didn't think he'd gotten since entering the house. Nao waited there a few minutes, then peeked out of the blinds to make sure the children were out of sight.

The small lie about never going to the safe house must be hiding bigger ones, and his men needed weapons.

Nao opened the kitchen cabinets and searched. Nothing terribly out of the ordinary, since it was, for all purposes, a yakuza household.

Nao went into his bedroom, but after a few minutes of shuffling toys around, he still found nothing.

He groaned and pushed back the racecar bed. He knocked on the wooden floorboards. One sounded off. He dug his fingers around the floorboard until it pressed open. Inside was a locked safe.

Guns, perhaps, or maybe cash.

Nao shook his head. It couldn't be money. He couldn't see Yori sitting on a chest full of cash without spending it on her kids. Unless she didn't know? She knew too much about her house not to. The key might be in Yori's room, and he could give the guns to Aki and Kohta.

He walked to the other side of the house. The girls' room was clear, which only left Yori's bedroom. He put his hand on the doorknob and turned, but it was locked. Something important had to be in there, because all the other rooms were open.

Nao groaned and banged his shoulder against the wall as the front door opened.

"Excuse me," Yori said, her arms crossed over her chest. "You have absolutely no business going into my bedroom."

CHAPTER 17

•••

NAO KEPT HIS hand on the doorknob. Yori's face twisted. She lowered her chin, and she glared at him, but Nao stood his ground.

"Since the Matsukawa and the Mafufugumi are going to be business partners, I wanted to check out the porn site," he said. "I figured you had a computer in your room, but it's locked."

"Of course I keep it locked. It's the only room where I can get some peace." She rubbed her elbow, her eyes darting to her kids bouncing around the house, then back to the door.

"Don't worry. I don't plan on disturbing anything. I just want to check out the site."

Like Nao had any idea how to look up a website. He'd seen Kohta use it, so it shouldn't be too difficult. Even when Nao had owed his tearoom, he'd contacted tea brokers over the phone and kept the books on paper before handing it over to the accountant his father had selected for him.

"I have a laptop you can use. That way you're not stuck in my

room to handle your business." She gave a small laugh.

Nao crossed his arms. Getting off on any porn Shinji directed would be impossible. "That won't be necessary."

"No worries. I had four kids. I know how it goes." She winked and turned toward Giichi. "Go get your sisters ready for bed. I'll be there to help in just a second."

"Then can I play Mario?"

"Did you study today?"

Giichi rubbed his green-and-blue striped socked foot into the wooden floor. "But Mom, it's a snow day."

Yori sighed. "Fine, but tomorrow you're studying for two hours as soon as you get up."

Her son padded away to his sisters as soon as Yori agreed. Nao's mother had had a difficult time conceiving him, so Nao had ended up being an only child. Sibling relationships were lost to him. Still, seeing Giichi interact with his younger sisters made Nao smile.

"Those train tracks can't get cleared fast enough," Yori mumbled.

"Are they usually cleared away by now?" Nao asked.

"It's hard to say. There's more snow coming tomorrow, so whatever progress they made will push it back."

"That's unfortunate."

"This time of year, it always happens. Here, hold him for me, and I'll grab that laptop for you."

Yori's movements were so fast that before he could reject the offer, the baby was already in his arms. She pulled a necklace over her head and unlocked the door.

"Yori, I don't really—"

"Look, he's smiling. You're a natural dad."

She squeezed past Nao, only opening the door wide enough for her to go in.

"I'll be just a second." She locked the door behind her.

Nao raised a brow. Something had to be in there she didn't want Nao to see.

He leaned in closer, and Yori's muffled voice could be heard through the door. He couldn't understand what she was saying. She was probably talking to herself with how frazzled she looked.

The baby wiggled in Nao's arms, pulling his attention away from the door. The baby was so squishy, and Nao half-expected to drop him and give him a brain disorder. Then the child opened its mouth and let out a cry.

Nao pushed the baby away from him. How could he get the kid to shut up? There was no way he could deal with children. The family name could die with him, and he wouldn't care.

"Haven't you been around a baby?" Yori asked as she slipped out of the bedroom.

Nao held out the baby. "Can you make it stop?"

She snickered and traded the laptop for her baby. She cooed at him, and in a few seconds, he stopped crying.

Nao rubbed his ear. "Thanks."

"He just wanted his mommy, didn't you?" She nuzzled the kid. "I got the website loaded for you and logged you in with the full-access membership. You'll get all the top-tier stuff."

"Thanks." Nao held up the laptop. "Do I need to do anything to get it going?"

The side of her mouth curled up. "Oh honey, you've been on

a computer before, haven't you?"

Nao narrowed his eyes. He wasn't incompetent.

"Of course I have," Nao lied. "I meant is there a password?"

"Nope. Just open it up, and it'll be on the page."

Nao nodded. "I see."

"Have a nice night, Mr. Murata."

Giichi stopped Nao on his path to his room. He stood there crossing his arms, his face squished and his lip pursed.

"What's wrong?" Nao asked.

"We were at the boss fight."

"I got some business to do first."

"But you said you'd play."

Nao rubbed the edge of the computer. "I'll help you defeat the boss tomorrow."

Giichi held out his pinkie. "Promise?"

"Promise." Nao wrapped his pinkie around Giichi's, and he gave their locked fingers a frim shake.

After that Giichi was satisfied and allowed him to pass.

Nao carried the laptop to his bedroom and propped it up on the racecar bed while he sat cross-legged on the futon. He lifted the top of the laptop, and the screen remained black.

It took a few minutes to figure out how to turn it on. Why couldn't they use a simple toggle on-and-off switch? Technology despised Nao. It was always on and so loud. He enjoyed the quiet once the TVs had been removed from headquarters even though it was replaced by the grumble of recruits. He'd even ordered the TVs out of the common areas in headquarters. It might've irritated the new recruits, but once the new ones came in, Nao didn't hear any more complaints.

He pushed the yellow flashing button, and the screen finally came to life. Images of naked women emerged.

Nao sighed.

He'd cared more about exploring Yori's room for whatever she was keeping hidden inside than checking out the site, but since he was already there, perhaps he'd find something interesting.

The front-page auto-refreshed every few minutes, posting the trending video next to a flashing banner. So many of the thumbnails had women in them. Nao had figured since Shinji was into men, there'd be at least a few videos of gay sex.

After a few minutes of failed searching, Nao clicked back to the home page, a new trending video popped up, but instead of a lady, the thumbnail showed a fully erect cock.

He clicked it open, and the video immediately got into the action. The man's hand encircled his length and jerked. His moans were delicious, but where the man's skin met skin was paper white. There were even white rings around parts of his thick cock. Then the man's hand rubbed along his head before trailing down. It reminded Nao of…

Aki?

Nao narrowed his eyes, and he leaned in closer to the screen. It wasn't like he'd memorized the pattern on Aki's hands as he made the morning tea for them, but it was uncanny.

"That's so hot, baby," Shinji's voice came from the video.

The shot panned up to Aki's face. He bit his lip, stifling another moan. He looked hot, but no matter how alluring it was, it made Nao's stomach churn.

Even Kohta had had the decency to ask if it was okay to be in one of Shinji's films.

Nao curled his hand into a fist and clicked off the video. Clearly, Aki thought he could do whatever he wanted.

Aki's moans ceased when Nao clicked off the video.

He poked around the site for a few minutes, diving deeper into the members-only area. He clicked open one of the videos with just a name listed. It loaded and clicked open. Then some five-year-old girl blinked on the screen then twirled around in a short dress. Nao clicked off as an adult man came into the shot.

Nao pushed the laptop away.

It might've been disgusting, but it wasn't enough to call off a whole alliance. Illegal porn was how a lot of yakuza made their money, and if Nao threw a fit about what the Mafufugumi were doing, it would lead to the Matsukawa dealing with a few more enemies.

CHAPTER 18

· · ·

THE LIGHTS CLICKED on. Aki blinked awake, his eyes stinging. Shit.

He'd slept with his contacts in again. Back home, he'd never be so forgetful, but Hokkaido covered all his routines underneath a blizzard of snow. No matter how much Aki wished things would happen his way, every step he took resulted in his failure.

"How could you do it?" Shinji asked.

Aki turned his head to Shinji's voice, getting an unfocused view of his blue boxer-briefs-clad body. Even blurry, his sculpted shoulders and arms had Aki unconsciously licking his lips. Aki rubbed his eyes, moving the lenses back into their proper place.

"What time is it?" Aki asked.

Aki reached for the nightstand, but his phone wasn't there. It must still be in his pants. Where were his pants?

Shinji bowed his head and softly shook it. "Why did you do it, Aki?"

"Do what?"

Shinji dragged himself to the bed and covered his hands with his face. "How could you use me like that?"

"What?" Aki placed a hand on Shinji's slumped shoulders. "I would never do that."

"Yeah, right." Shinji's voice cracked.

Aki sat up, the sheets falling away from his naked body. He wrapped his arms around Shinji, and when he relaxed, Aki pressed his cheek against Shinji's back.

"Sshh, tell me what's going on." Aki kissed Shinji's neck.

He pointed to the laptop in the corner on the floor. "It crashed. It's been down for hours."

Aki held on to his breath and squeezed Shinji a little tighter.

Sure, after they'd had the best sex Aki could remember having, Shinji had fallen asleep. It made up for the session he couldn't remember and allowed him to use the laptop. Aki had then taken the opportunity to try reaching home again. He'd paused Shinji's video upload and opened a new tab. The new page had flashed white, and the mouse turned from a pointer to the loading circle. With each passing minute, Aki's eyes had darted from the screen to make sure Shinji was still asleep. Aki needed to get a message to Kurosawa. Shinji would understand.

But after a whole half hour had passed, the new tab had remained a blank page. Aki had closed the tab and tried once more, but still nothing. Eventually he'd given up, restarted the video upload, and gone to bed.

Aki bit his lip and squeezed Shinji's bicep. "Did the internet go out or something?"

"Why are you lying to me when I've never lied to you?" Shinji clutched Aki's hand. "You tried to pause my uploads. I told you it wouldn't work. Why didn't you believe me?"

Aki's cheeks grew hot, and he pulled away from Shinji, but he kept hold of Aki's hand. Shinji's strength outdid Aki. He knew stopping Shinji's videos was wrong, but he had to do it.

"Why?" Shinji said again.

Aki had a duty to Nao and the family. That duty came before the relationship he was forming with Shinji. He was a yakuza. He should understand. A chill ran up Aki's spine as Shinji's grip tightened, but he took a deep breath and squeezed Shinji's hand.

"I had no other choice," Aki said, his voice coming out as clear and crisp as a crease in a paper.

"I told you how important it was to keep the upload going, and you fucking tried to pause it."

"There was no other option. I'm sorry, but I had to try to get word back home. They have no idea why it's taking us so long and I need to know what's going on there."

"They could even turn on a TV and see that the whole island has been one big blizzard the past few days. Watanabe has told them the situation. You guys are our allies."

Even in the middle of the argument, Shinji clutched onto Aki's hand, not in anger but in desperation.

"I'm so dead." Shinji's eyes were like a teacup about to be overfilled. "I'll be lucky if they give my ashes to family."

Aki inwardly grimaced. He hadn't meant for it to get to the point where Shinji would cry.

Shinji and all the Mafufugumi were their allies. Watanabe might've been a dick for changing his mind, but the members of the Mafufugumi had showed him nothing but kindness. The small side quest to buy the prostitutes was a standard request.

"I'm sorry," Aki said. "Nao's been furious that I haven't been able to contact home."

"Yori has internet at her house. He could contact them there anytime."

Aki looked away. The pain inside his chest when he looked at Shinji's eyes grew too overwhelming.

"Nao doesn't know how to use the internet," Aki whispered.

"What the fuck?"

"He's a huge technopho—"

"So because he'll piss himself if he gets near a computer, you put my balls on the line. When Watanabe finds out what happened…" Shinji trailed off, his chin trembling.

Aki bit his lip and placed his other hand on the one Shinji clasped and gave it a squeeze. The blue glow of the computer scene bathed the room in an unnatural hue. The lingering musk of their sex clung to the sheets, and the herbs the Russians used for their dinner wafted in the air. The room couldn't feel further away from Kyoto.

"You can just tell him the computer died," Aki suggested. "It happens all the time."

Shinji shook his head. "No, you don't get it. The site is the lifeblood of the Mafufugumi. That's how we make most of our funds."

Aki raised a brow. Keeping the entire funds of a family alive by a single business was financial suicide. The Matsukawa had their hands in dozens of businesses. It only made sense, especially with all the anti-yakuza laws.

Shinji sniffed and whipped his eyes with the back of his free hand. "And everything is so tight after what happened."

Aki blinked. "After what happened?"

"It was supposed to be an easy exchange. Everything was going according to plan, then Murata fucked everything up."

Shinji slumped over, burying his head into the blankets. Aki rubbed his hand along Shinji's back. The first touch got a sharp gasp of breath, but then Shinji settled into the touch. If Watanabe was even half as critical as Nao was when it came to people not meeting his expectations, then Aki held no doubt Shinji's words were true. Aki swallowed. And it was all his fault.

"Remember how you said you wanted to be a film director," Aki said, keeping a light tone in his voice, but Shinji never replied. "After this is all over, why not come to Kyoto? I can set you up with a job at the film studio."

Shinji shook his head and spoke into the blanket. "Murata would never allow that."

"He'd never know. It's not like he visits the studio. Since I'm his secretary, I can give an order and people will assume it's from him."

"You'd really do that for me?"

"Of course. I understand how rough it could be trying to do what's good for the family and putting yourself second." The words slipped out of Aki, but hearing himself say it out loud…

It had to be true, or else he wouldn't have said it. Aki closed his eyes and listened to the sound of Shinji's breath returning to a steady pace.

Aki had never imagined being with a guy who cried his eyes

out over something so small, but Shinji wanted him, and in Aki's heart, he finally felt like he belonged. All the feeling he'd ever gotten from Nao was that the man wished they'd never met.

He'd been putting Nao and the family first since joining the Matsukawa. Then when Aki had finally started acting in his own interests and gone with Shinji, Nao had become furious. But the Matsukawa were his family. Without them, he'd have no one.

It wasn't true anymore, though. Aki opened his eyes and kissed along Shinji's spine. Shinji cared about him, and when he'd looked into his eyes, Aki could tell Shinji shared the same feelings. He'd never felt as needed before as he did consoling Shinji.

Aki still had a duty to the Matsukawa, but they couldn't be the reason for his existence. It would be better if he stopped his misguided infatuation with Nao. It was for the betterment of the family.

Aki sighed and lay down beside Shinji. His eyes were closed, but a half smile crossed his face. Aki pulled Shinji close, chest against chest, the lingering scent of sex still fresh on their skin.

"It's settled, then," Aki said. "You can tell Watanabe that Father Murata wanted to use the internet. You couldn't say no to him."

"That's perfect. He couldn't get mad at me for following the order of a godfather."

"See, you'll be all right," Aki said, but more to reassure himself than anything.

"You really mean what you said about you finding me a job at the film studio in Kyoto?"

"Of course."

"So that means we're a real thing now."

Aki nodded. "Yeah."

Shinji smashed their lips together. The welcomed kiss pushed away any doubt Aki had in him. Shinji was the right choice. Aki might've not really known much about Shinji other than he bottomed as good as he topped, but they would share more than sex in time.

"You're so fucking hot," Shinji whispered in Aki's ear before playfully nipping it.

CHAPTER 19

◆ ◆ ◆

HALF-ASLEEP, AKI REACHED out to snuggle against Shinji but was met with nothing but a cold bed. He groaned and sat up. Shinji must've had more filming to do.

Aki stretched before getting out of bed. He rubbed his stinging eyes and moved his lenses back into place. He probably should grab the rest of his things from his own room. Then he'd finally get his contacts case to avoid the sting of sleeping with them in.

Maybe it was for the best he didn't leave. Kohta probably would've found that opportunity to come out of his room, and he'd have to deal with even more of his lewd comments about him and Shinji.

His suitcase had all his clean clothes, and the clothes he had strewn about the room were dirty and wrinkled. Even the thought of putting them on to go back to his room made him grimace. He could maybe just slip on the underwear and cross the hall, but all the Russians were probably out in the living room, and it seemed so unprofessional since it was already in the afternoon.

"Your memory is worse than I thought it would be. Must be all the Russian vodka." Nao's voice was loud enough to be heard through the walls.

Fuck.

Two days in a row he wasn't up and prepared with a cup of tea for when Nao arrived.

How could Aki sleep through Nao entering? Why hadn't Shinji or Kohta woken him?

Aki got dressed, hoping the lingering sweat of sex didn't cling to his skin as much as he imagined. He walked out, running his fingers through his hair.

Nao was in the living room chatting with Bow Tie. Ivan still lay on the sofa, but his eyes weren't open like usual. A washcloth was on his head. He must be getting worse. Shinji sat in a chair next to Nao, clearly there for translation purposes only.

Nao's gaze darted to Aki, who gave a formal bow and mumbled a good afternoon, but by the time Aki got up from the bow, Nao had looked away. Aki pressed his lips together and slipped into the kitchen. He set the water boiler to the perfect temperature for oolong tea.

Shinji translated what Bow Tie said. "He's worried about Ivan dying."

"If you had stuck to the original agreement, then you wouldn't be in this situation," Nao said.

Aki half listened but then grew more and more focused on

making Nao's tea. What mood was Nao in? Did he need more a strong-astringency oolong for dealing with the Russians and their unending talk about Ivan's near death, or something lighter to refresh the mood? He'd only brought a handful of different teas, and none of them fit.

It only took a few minutes to bring the water to the right temperature and warm up the pot of tea. He grabbed the cream oolong tea, knowing it was Nao's favorite. He could use something he enjoyed while he discussed issues with the Russians.

With the teapot warmed, Aki filled the wire basket inside the pot with the tight balls of rolled tea leaves. The light scent of butter filled his nose as he poured the water over the leaves.

The conversation between Nao and Bow Tie grew more heated, but Shinji somehow managed to keep the calm.

Aki walked to Nao's side, bringing the teapot and cup with him. He bowed and followed the usual steps of taking the wire basket and putting it beside the pot. Nao enjoyed the look of the uncurled leaves. He then poured the cup for Nao.

Nao leaned in close enough that Aki could feel his hot breath on the side of his face. Aki smiled. At least Nao didn't seem too mad that Aki hadn't had his tea ready the moment he'd entered the Mafufugumi warehouse.

After filling the cup, Aki caught Nao's nostrils flaring and a crease forming between his eyebrows. Aki gulped.

"I humbly beg your forgiveness for my tardiness," Aki said, laying on his Kyoto accent thick.

Nao said nothing and grabbed the cup. He brought it to his lips, and the cringe grew deeper.

Aki's heart leapt into his throat. He'd made it like he usually had. Sure, the water in Kyoto was different, but Nao had liked the tea yesterday, or at least had never said anything.

Nao sighed.

"Aki," Nao said.

"Yes, Father Murata?"

"Don't waste my tea leaves if you can't prepare my tea correctly," Nao hissed.

Aki blinked. "I-I—"

Time slowed, and Aki stood frozen as Nao turned over the teacup he held. The green liquid spilled onto the carpeted floor. The light butter scent soured in Aki's nose. Aki's jaw dropped, but Nao's face remained as blank. He grabbed the teapot and poured the unwanted tea in front of Aki's socked feet.

"Don't bother making my tea again," Nao said. "I'll be doing it myself from now on."

CHAPTER 20

•　•　•

THE SPILLING TEA echoed in Aki's ears as the world plummeted into a bottomless void around him. Everything inside of Aki wanted to protest his demotion, but he knew he shouldn't. Yet with his world breaking around him, how could he not defend himself?

He opened his mouth to protest, but no words came out. Pain welled in his chest, and his hands shook. Aki cursed himself. He was with Nao, and beside him, Aki had had nothing to fear. Aki swallowed the lump in his throat and tried to speak again.

"You're dismissed, Mr. Hisona," Nao said, not giving Aki the chance to speak.

Nao used his last name? He'd never called him by his last name. Why would he suddenly change?

Aki winced, then bowed to avoid Nao's intense gaze, but it was impossible. His heart thrashed in his chest. Aki stifled a heavy cry. When Aki straightened from his bow, Nao remained transfixed. His eyes were locked on him in an unavoidable stare.

Nao's eyes hadn't held their usual look of restrained desire but pierced through Aki's very being, like Nao was about to slice his stomach open and bathe in his blood. Nao would do it. Aki had no doubt about it.

Aki had always felt immune to the sheer ruthless power Nao possessed. He'd always been so careful and restrained around him. But trapped within Nao's gaze, Aki knew how wrong he was.

"I said get out of my sight!" Nao slammed his fist against the table.

Aki jumped, then staggered away. His feet led him to the front door, where he grabbed his coat and slid on his shoes.

His dress shoes crunched underneath the freshly fallen snow. The chill didn't sting. In fact, Aki welcomed the numbness to dull his aching heart.

Maybe the water was different. The storm might've messed up the pipes and brought up some different minerals in the water.

"What could've pissed him off so much?" Aki mumbled to himself, stepping farther away from the warehouse.

Aki replayed the scene in his head, but nothing could explain Nao's reaction. Aki had made and presented the tea perfectly. Aki stopped, his feet sinking into the snow.

Nao had smelled the sex on him. There was no other explanation. Nao wasn't mad about the tea. He was mad because Aki couldn't strike a balance between his personal life and his duty to the family. Nao had blamed it on the tea in order for Aki to save face in front of everyone. He had put the family second, and Nao had seen it.

Aki ran his fingers through his hair. How could he be so stupid to not realize it right away? Aki pulled his cell phone out of his pocket. Maybe outside, he could get reception and prove he put his devotion to the family first. Nao would see he was a loyal servant. Aki could do everything Nao needed and still keep a social life.

Aki held up the cell phone, trying to get a signal. One bar popped up. Maybe if he moved a little higher up the hill, he'd be able to get something stronger. Getting ahold of Kurosawa was the only way to prove to Nao that he was able to be the person he wanted. He could still be worthy of being Nao's secretary.

Maybe Aki was wrong about everything. He'd spent so long wanting him that he hadn't realized that Nao wasn't feeling anywhere close to the same.

He'd projected his own desires for Nao into everything he did. It wasn't like Nao was warming up any more since that one kiss.

Aki sighed. He had the start of something with Shinji anyway. Once they were in Kyoto, they could date properly, and Aki could learn more than what sex positions suited them best. Aki shook his head. He'd been so desperate for needing to be desired that he hadn't gotten to know anything about Shinji.

He held up the phone again.

Two bars. It was worth a try. Nao needed to know what was happening back home, especially since Kurosawa had made Aki lie about everything being fine. He called, but it couldn't connect.

"There's bound to be service somewhere." Aki groaned.

Snow fell around him as Aki continued his walk, guided by

whether a new bar flashed on the phone or not. Once he got three bars, he tried calling again, but the signal fell.

He sighed and looked over his shoulder, but he couldn't see anything but the blanket of white, falling snow. The warehouse was nowhere in sight.

Shit.

Aki turned around again.

Fuck.

He was lost.

Aki pulled up the collar of his coat to break the swirling wind. He wasn't sure how much time had passed, but he knew he had walked in a straight line. He just needed to walk back in a straight line. He'd be fine.

His steps steadied as the air flurried with snow. He rubbed his hands over his arms as the chill inside him stretched to his limbs and bit at his fingertips. He swallowed. Even his contacts felt like they were freezing to his eyeballs. His ears hurt with the howl of the wind so strong it was deafening. His hand shook as he checked the phone again.

The deep cold dulled his core.

He still hadn't gotten ahold of Kurosawa, so he'd have nothing to redeem himself in Nao's eyes.

Aki's foot caught on something, and he tumbled to the ground, the snow clinging to his face and lips. He brushed it away, extremities too numb to even feel the contact.

His fall swept back a layer of snow, and Aki squinted, not believing what he saw. He stood and took a step forward, and his eyes grew wide.

A frozen hand stuck out from the snow.

CHAPTER 21

• • •

AKI FELL BACK, and the snow flurried around him. He shook his head. It couldn't be right. It had to be some strange kind of snow blindness.

He rubbed his eyes and crawled to the small hand. The fingertips were black, while farther down the arm was the gray color of death. Snowflakes clung to the fine hairs on the arm. The crisp scent of snow lingered in the back of his nose where human decay should've been.

Aki swallowed and reached out to touch the arm. It was as cold as Nao's feelings toward him, and just as small. Aki's hand was almost double the size. His hands and arms grew so numb he couldn't even tell where the snow ended and he began.

He dug out the forearm and then the shoulders. He picked up his speed as he exposed the neck, the heat returning to his limbs driving the cold to sting once more. His quick inhales and exhales of breath were the only sound. He got to the face and brushed back the last layer of snow.

It was a little girl.

She had to be no more than ten. She stared up at Aki with pale green eyes. Snow clung to her eyelashes, and the tip of her nose was as black as a yakuza suit.

Aki's hand covered his gaping mouth.

"Holy shit."

He shook his head and dug out more of her body. She had to have some kind of identification in her pocket. Aki dug more of the corpse out of the foot of snow, but past her neck, there was nothing but blue skin. She was naked.

Aki swallowed and clung to his coat.

Hypothermia did make people do funny things. He'd heard stories of people taking off their clothes in the middle of winter.

Parts of her were under a foot of snow, but other parts, like her hand, were still exposed to the elements. There was no way to know how long she'd been there.

She must've gotten lost playing outside and frozen to death. But there were so few people in the village; wouldn't someone be looking for her? Someone had to be looking for her. Even knowing that their daughter was dead was better than not knowing what happened.

It was his duty as a yakuza to help anyone who was helpless. If he found the girl's parents, then Nao would see the part of the Matsukawa oath to be chivalrous as an absolute duty even away from Kyoto.

Aki couldn't go to the police. He was a yakuza; the lazy bastards would blame her death on him for whatever reason. He could go knocking on one of the villagers' doors. In such a small town, a missing girl had to be on everyone's lips. He stood up and gulped down his breath. He could show the parents directly, and there wouldn't be a need for any cops to be involved.

The cold air stung his lungs. He'd find a house soon enough.

CHAPTER 22

. ♦ .

AS SOON AS Nao opened the door of Yori's home, the scraping of dog nails against the wooden floor sent Nao grimacing. He kicked off one of his shoes, but by then the dogs were already there.

"Down!" Yori yelled, but of course the pack didn't listen.

The pony-sized malamute jumped up, his front paws on Nao's shoulders. It licked at his face. Nao gagged as the dog's pungent, rotten-fish-like breath slammed his face.

"I said down, Kimi! Leave Mr. Murata alone." She grabbed hold of the dog's collar and pulled her down.

With the largest member of the pack taken care of, it left the two smaller dogs to weave in and out of Nao's legs, while the two medium-sized dogs ran in circles around Yori. How could dogs be so needy? He'd only been gone for a few hours. It wasn't like they were abandoned. The house was filled with people for them to play with.

Cats were so much easier to deal with.

He sighed and waited for Yori to get a handle on the mutts. With each minute outside Kyoto, more of his strength to deal with everything left him. Kyoto ignited his blood and gave him life, but the ice rock of Hokkaido exhausted him more each day.

Giichi rounded the corner, thankfully getting the attention of the dogs.

"Do you want me to take them outside?" he asked.

"No. There's supposed to be more snow. Just leave them in your sisters' room."

Giichi ran down the hall, getting all the dogs to chase him. Nao closed his eyes.

Another snowstorm. It meant more time stuck between a dog kennel and a whore house filled with Russians ready to knock him off.

Yori grabbed Nao's boots and put them on the top of the shoe rack by the entryway.

"You wouldn't happen to have been a nurse before you met Watanabe?" Nao asked.

"Sometimes I feel like I am." She laughed. "Did something happen?"

Nao shrugged. "One of the Russians had an accident with a knife."

"Oh my, that can't be good."

"I stabbed him in a place where he'd be fine getting help by morning, but then the trains never came, and they keep on getting fucking delayed."

"You st-stabbed someone?"

Nao narrowed his eyes. "You do know what Watanabe does?"

"I mean yes, I just…" She looked away. "You're so patient with Giichi."

So she wasn't used to the gritty details of Watanabe's business. Nao shook his head. "I only attack when someone deserves it."

"I can understand being frustrated with them," she said under her breath.

"The Russians piss you off, too, then?"

"You know what? I'll make some soup tonight. Maybe it'll help."

Nao leaned against the door. "Letting me borrow a gun would be a better help than making soup."

"I don't have any weapons."

Nao laughed. "Really? There's a locked gun case underneath Giichi's bed."

"What?"

"You didn't know about that?" Nao crossed his arms.

"Of course not."

"My father kept some under my bed, too. Must be a common godfather thing. So where's the key?"

"Watanabe has the key."

Nao took a step closer. "You did know there was a safe there. What else are you lying to me about? Shinji told me you teach some of the girls some Japanese."

"Sometimes." Yori took a step back.

"But you said you weren't allowed down there."

Yori laughed. "You're not going to tell Watanabe, are you? I think it's important for those women to know at least a few words. They need to know what's going on."

"I don't care about Watanabe. I care that you were lying to me."

"It won't happen again."

Giichi walked in, his nose pinched. "Mom, the baby needs changing."

"A mom's work is never done."

She walked away. Giichi looked up at Nao with a wide smile on his face. Nao's muscles loosened, and he realized he couldn't do anything else when it came to Yori.

"You promised you'd beat the boss with me," Giichi said.

"I did, didn't I?"

"And it was a pinkie promise. You can't go against those."

Nao nodded. He'd keep it, since having a friendly relationship with Giichi might come in handy at some point.

"Let's make a pot of tea and then we'll play. You know how to make tea?" Nao asked.

"Mom makes it all the time."

"Does she do it with those awful bags or with loose tea?"

"Loose tea?"

Nao cracked a smile. "I'll show you how to make it right. Hopefully there's leaves somewhere."

Giichi followed Nao to the kitchen and jumped on the counter as Nao filled the water boiler.

"See, all the different teas like a specific temperature, and since we don't know what kind we'll find, let's set it for the lowest one. Here, you want to do it?"

Nao pointed as Giichi clicked over for the temperature for oolong. A bit of wishful thinking on Nao's part. It was a shame

Aki was growing too distracted getting his hole fucked to do his job. Nao needed to remember to take the tea leaves away from him the next time Nao traveled to the warehouse.

"Good. Now we just have to find some tea," Nao said.

He opened one of the cabinets, but there was nothing but a bunch of tools. The echo of a baby crying made its way into the kitchen. Yori would be busy for a while.

"Do you ever go into Mommy's room?" Nao asked.

"Sometimes."

"Only sometimes?"

Giichi opened the cabinet next to him, while Nao opened one of the lower cabinets and found a few beaten-up boxes of tea. Nao grabbed them and put them on the counter beside Giichi.

"These are dusty," Giichi said.

Nao opened one of the boxes and pulled out a teabag. "Yeah, there's dust in here, too."

"Mom likes coffee more."

"She needs all the caffeine she can get with you guys." Nao dug back in the cabinet, pushing aside some plasticware. "Maybe your mom keeps the good tea in her room."

Giichi shook his head. "We're not allowed to go there anymore."

"Hm?" Nao tried to sound bored. "Did something happen?"

"She locked the door."

"Ahh." Nao stood. "Did you guys break something?"

Giichi crossed his arms. "No."

He ruffled the kid's hair. "That's good. I used to break all kinds of stuff when I was mad."

"Really?"

"I once broke a very expensive tea bowl."

"Your mom must've been mad."

"My dad was fucking pissed."

Giichi's mouth dropped, and Nao raised a brow.

"You said a bad word."

"I did, didn't I?" Nao leaned in close to Giichi. "Let's keep it a secret between us. I won't want your mom mad at me, and we can't play Mario."

Giichi nodded.

Nao squatted and reached a little deeper into the cabinet. "How long have you been locked out of Mom's room?"

"Two weeks."

"That's a long time, huh?"

"Yeah."

"What do you think is in there?"

Giichi tapped his finger on his lips. "There was a loud noise at the door, and when I went to see, she told me to go back to my room. It's been locked since."

Who would show up at the door that Yori would want to hide so much?

"Ah! Here we go." Nao reached into the back of the cabinet and pulled out a dusty tin of loose green tea.

He explained to Giichi why the leaves were better than bagged, which were filled with dust and twigs. It almost felt like he was back in his teahouse. Nao stood. It had been so much easier back then.

Nao poured some water into a teapot to heat it up when Yori came back.

"You're making tea," she said.

"My usual guy messed up."

Yori narrowed her eyes and glanced toward Giichi.

"Get off the counter so Mommy can make soup for Mr. Murata's sick friend," Yori said.

Nao chuckled. "He's going to need a lot more than soup."

"Mama's soup cures anything." Giichi jumped down.

"Before you start, get me the laptop with the membership loaded. I wanted to check out a few more things."

"Anything." Yori began to walk down the hall, and Nao followed. "It's okay. I can bring it back to you."

"It's fine."

She squeezed into the bedroom again, and even though it was dark, Nao could make out someone on the bed. Nao leaned closer, but Yori slammed the door. Maybe she had her own side guy, and the snow was keeping him there.

Nao pressed his lips together. There would be no reason for her to keep him there for two weeks. Maybe she just didn't make her bed, and the sheets looked like a person.

The door opened again, and Nao wasn't able to get a better view. He thanked her and took the laptop and pot of tea and headed for his room.

"Hey, you said we'd beat the boss." Giichi stretched out his arms and touched each wall, blocking Nao's path.

Nao smiled. "Remember I said after tea."

"Okay, but right after."

"I promise."

Giichi allowed Nao to pass. He needed to make sure to play

the game with the kid or else all trust he had in Nao would be gone.

Nao popped open the computer and clicked through the porn videos. He'd probably get a full-length movie of Shinji and Aki with the way he'd reeked of sex. It was disgusting how distracted Aki could get. If Nao had known before, he would've never made him his secretary. He needed to figure how to balance his work with his stupid love affair with an idiot.

Nao clicked open the old video of Aki and stared. Aki's moans were so delicious, but then Shinji talked, and it made Nao want to gag. He scrolled down, and a comment section loaded.

Nao poured a cup of tea and read through each of the comments. Each comment grew more vulgar than the one before, but it was clear they all wanted more from the two-toned freak. Nao shook his head. Good to know if Nao fired Aki, he could be okay taking up a career in exploitation porn.

The video replayed, and Nao scrolled back up to the top. He enlarged the video and then paused it as the camera switched to the wide view as it panned over. It didn't look like the studio Shinji had showed him. The way Aki looked at the camera seemed off. It almost reminded Nao of the far-off gaze with which Shinya had looked at him on that night.

Nao closed the video. It wasn't his business what Aki was doing.

He came back to the main page. Shinya? Nao rubbed his eyes. Of course it wasn't Shinya, but the still image of Kohta from behind jumbled his thoughts like a snowflake in a blizzard. If it wasn't for Kohta's love of wearing the tackiest clothes in Japan, he'd be almost a perfect double.

Even after all these years, the pain was like a raw wound, especially at night. When Nao slept, Shinya always returned, but the more the Koreans drew close to the city, the more Saehyun joined him too.

Nao lay down and stared at the burn on his wrist. The blood thirst trapped inside was because of that night in Tokyo. It was the only reason Kyoto was still safe. Nao swallowed. It was silly to hold onto his feelings and sillier to hold a jealous grudge over Aki. Of course he'd find someone who could return his feelings.

Nao had the city. He didn't need anyone else.

He lay there. For how long he wasn't sure… minutes… hours, but he slowly slipped off his suit and pulled on his yukata. He needed to help beat a Mario boss.

CHAPTER 23
• • •

AKI HAD NEVER known there were so many stars. The street-lights of Kyoto hid so many of them, but the sky above the little village exploded with the twinkling. Aki stumbled, staring up to them, landing face first in the snow. He closed his eyes and rubbed his head.

"Don't get distracted. You got-gotta get back," Aki mumbled to himself.

When the snow had fallen again, Aki had gotten turned around. He could barely keep track of where he was let alone find any of the villagers' houses. At one point, he knew he'd been out for three hours, but a while ago, his phone had died and he'd lost all track of time. His arms had grown numb ages ago, and every few steps, he tripped over his feet.

Aki swallowed. The warehouse had to be somewhere close. He'd been heading in the right direction. All the white had made him tired, but he knew he couldn't go to sleep until he made it back.

His uneasy steps continued, and when Aki blinked, a building popped into view. Had it always been there? He ran closer, his breath coming in long, winded pants. With each of his strides, his legs weighed more and drained more of the energy out of him.

The structure ended up not being the warehouse he'd hoped for but the train station. So much snow covered the roof it looked like the wooden support beams would snap, but it was the only protection from the elements Aki had. He stepped onto the platform, a light dusting of snow on the benches and concrete floor. Even if one side was open to the cold, it was better than nothing. Aki knew the way to the train station. It was just when he tried to remember, his thoughts jumbled them up. If he warmed up, he should figure it out.

The ramen vending machine still hummed, and the little light was like its own shining star.

Aki dug in his pocket and pulled out a few yen coins. He fed them to the machine, and in a minute's time, steam spilled out of the glass protection. He opened the case and pulled out the thick plasticware protecting the ramen. The bowl warmed his blue hands, and the sweet smell of pork wafted to his nose and made his stomach grumble.

He brushed away the snow from the bench and brought the bowl to his lips and slurped it. The miso broth curled his toes. It was so delicious. Each slurp brought new exciting flavors of pork, corn, and toasted sesame seeds.

After he finished half the bowl, he wiped his mouth with his sleeve. He closed his eyes and smiled.

When he was a child, his grandfather had been a vending machine operator. Their little apartment would be filled with the plastic ramen bowls as Aki's grandfather gave directions in his broken elementary Japanese. His grandmother would answer in the elegant Kyoto dialect expected from an ex-geiko. They'd all become chefs, those days placing the dried ingredients in each plastic ramen tub. Those days his grandfather smiled the most and would come home early enough to play with Aki. By the time Aki grew old enough to switch between the two dialects without trouble, the old-style vending machines had vanished, and his family were no longer chefs.

Aki sighed and swirled the half-empty bowl. What would they think of what he had become? They had always stressed hard work, but here he was in the yakuza.

Aki closed his eyes and imagined his grandfather sharing the bench with him, sipping his own ramen bowl. Yet when Aki opened his eyes, his *halbi* seemed more real than ever before. He smiled at Aki. Even in the days before his death, his smile was infectious.

"As long as you're not hurting anyone," Halbi said.

Aki wiped the tears from his eyes and looked away.

"Did they deserve it at least?"

"He was trying to frame me for murder," Aki said in Korean. "So he deserved it."

"I mean, I did do it—by accident. He pulled out a knife and then there was—"

Aki stopped talking once he met his grandfather's eyes. "I'm sorry. I didn't mean to disappoint you."

Halbi shook his head. "I take it that's not the suit of a businessman, is it?"

"It was so hard after you died. Granny followed soon after. Mom didn't really want to take me in. She barely spoke to me and was out drinking more than she was home. One night she stumbled in, and I was crying, clutching onto your photo. She snatched it from me and ripped it apart, saying I was too old do cry. Mom didn't bother taking care of me. I had no one and—and—" Aki gulped down a breath of cold air, stinging his lungs.

"We did the best we could with her. We knew how to do it better with you."

"I tried to do good. I really did. I worked at a company but got fired for screwing up. Everyone I knew was joining the yakuza. They gave me a home when I had none. I finally felt like I belonged."

"Hmmm."

Aki shut his eyes, and his chin dipped to his chest. "It was so hard when you guys were gone. I missed you so much."

"Remember the good times, Aki, before I got sick."

A heavy weight pressed on his shoulders and gave a squeeze. A flash of memories flashed at once before Aki's eyes. Watching his grandmother teaching a few girls dance at a studio while he watched. How Halbi once caught a huge fish in the lake, and for the first time he'd gone to bed stuffed. The day grandmother taught him how to fold his first crane because he'd come back the first day of school crying because the other kids made fun of his hands. Then how the ramen bowls dwindled down until they only took up a table. The dance lessons when from a studio to a park to a single girl in their cramped apartment. Halbi's coughing began soon after...

When Aki finally opened his eyes, nothing but snow covered the bench beside him. Aki's hand clutched into a fist.

He tried to think of the way back to the warehouse from a few days ago, but all the events grew foggy. The more he thought about it, the more confusing all the events became. Maybe if he lay down, he'd be able to think of the way back.

Aki's eyelids grew heavy. Aki's head hit the bench with a thud.

CHAPTER 24

· · ·

"AKI!" SHINJI'S VOICE pierced through the darkness.

Aki tried to open his eyes, but they grew heavy, and a voice inside told him it wasn't worth it. His time would be better spent sleeping. Why was Shinji so loud, anyway? Aki groaned. Ten more minutes wouldn't be too bad. Nao would understand, but Shinji kept shaking him.

"What were you thinking? You've been stuck out here for hours!" Shinji screamed.

"Hmm?"

Shinji grabbed Aki's hands and rubbed them together. "Shit, you're blue."

Aki forced his eyes open, but everything was so bright and he was so tired. He felt weightless as Shinji picked him up in his arms and carried him away. Heat radiated off Shinji, and even though it almost hurt, Aki became drawn toward it. He buried his head in the nook of Shinji's neck and breathed in his scent of cooked cabbage.

"You're gonna be okay, baby. I got you now. Let's get you warm. You'll be fine." Shinji kept on repeating the words over and over.

The warehouse door slammed shut behind Shinji. Heat pinpricked Aki's skin like he he'd been thrown into a furnace.

"Good, you found him," Kohta said. "I thought one of the Russians took you out."

Aki blinked. What was Kohta saying?

Kohta squeezed Aki's shoulder. "I couldn't begin to imagine how I'd tell Murata you died wandering around in the snow like that."

"I was lucky to find him when I did. Another hour out there, and he probably wouldn't have made it."

The pinpricks of heat made Aki's skin itch, but through the pain, the words Shinji and Kohta said started to become clear.

"Is he going to be okay?" Kohta asked.

Shinji sucked in a breath. "His fingers aren't black, so that's good. I still need to see about getting him warmed up though."

Aki's thoughts were still hazy, but he realized enough that Shinji was taking him to the bedroom. The soft blue light of Shinji's laptop made it easier for Aki to keep his eyes open.

Shinji put Aki down on the bed and gave him a kiss. It was gentle at first but then more demanding. His hand traced Aki's jaw until he opened up, allowing Shinji's tongue inside. The heat drew Aki in. He could breathe in Shinji's breath, and it lit a fire inside.

"Let's get you warmed up, babe," Shinji said.

Aki grabbed the blanket. Even though the warmth hurt his skin, he still needed it. But then Shinji kissed his lips again. His heat was better than any sheet. Aki closed his eyes. Of course, it was Shinji who saved him and not Nao. Nao didn't care.

"You know the easiest way to warm someone up." Shinji smiled.

"Shinji," Aki breathed out and pulled him closer.

He pulled back Aki's jacket collar and nipped at his neck.

"I want to record it," Shinji whispered.

Aki's cheeks grew hot and he shook his head.

Shinji pulled back. "Why are you so embarrassed again?"

"Please don't."

"I didn't record it last time. So let me do it this one."

Shinji leaned back, rubbing his ass against Aki's crotch, and began to unbutton Aki's coat. He let out a small moan, and Aki thrust his hips up at him. He couldn't bear it. He needed more of Shinji's heat. It was almost scary.

"Please, Aki," Shinji asked, pushing open Aki's coat. "You're so beautiful. I want to have something to beat off to when you're back in Kyoto."

Aki would be lying to himself if he denied that the thought of Shinji watching the video of what they did together once he was back home was a little bit of a turn-on.

"Shin…"

Shinji stripped off Aki's jacket and nipped at Aki's neck. He wanted to devour the heat of his mouth and let it consume him.

"Your body is so addictive."

Aki's hands snaked underneath Shinji's shirt and tried to

pinch at his nipples, but his fingers could not bend that way.

"You'll let me record, right?" Shinji asked again. "You have nothing to be embarrassed about. It's just for me."

"You're such a perv." Aki looked away.

"But I'm your perv."

Aki's fingers trailed up Shinji's leg until they reached the heat pulsing from his cock trapped under the fabric of his pants.

"You talk too much," Aki said.

"I'll shut up if you let me record."

Aki groaned. "Fine."

Shinji jumped up and messed around with the camera he had on his dresser.

"Are you ready?" Shinji asked.

"I thought you said you wouldn't talk if I let you record."

Shinji laughed and stripped off his coat. Just the way Shinji looked at him with a wanting expression made Aki want to lend Shinji his body to do whatever he wanted with.

Aki shivered with anticipation. Shinji smiled, cupping Aki's hand and helping him move it. Their mouths met again, and Aki closed his eyes, intensifying the heat. It was everything Aki wanted in a kiss. He could feel it reach inside with a drilling heat that made his toes curl. There was nothing more Aki could ever ask for.

"Nao," Aki moaned when they parted.

Shinji stared at him and Aki looked away.

"I'm sorry," he whispered. "I didn't mean…"

"Don't worry. When I'm done, you'll only want to say my name."

CHAPTER 25

. . .

THE SOUP YORI made probably froze on the way to the Mafu-fugumi's warehouse, but still Nao carried it downhill. She had wrapped the plastic container in a plum-purple fabric with white cranes. As it swung with each of Nao's steps, it was like the cranes took flight.

The choice of cloth resembled a kimono one of the Kyoto geiko would wear. Another thing to add to the list of things he missed about Kyoto—the geiko teahouses. He'd always stopped by weekly to see Yuiko, but with the delay, he'd missed a visit. Next time, he'd tell her how a seven-year-old kicked his butt at every video game franchise Nao knew.

Nao doubted the soup would do Ivan any good, but if anything, it might lower the tension. It wasn't like Nao knew they were going to get snowed in. Then he would've done something more superficial like slicing through his cheek or hacking off a few fingers.

After yesterday's blizzard, Yori had said there wasn't supposed to be any snow the next few days. If everything went in their favor, the tracks should be cleared and they could head home by tomorrow morning. Then Aki and Shinji would have to put their little production on hold.

Nao's free hand curled into a fist. There had been another video of them uploaded in the morning, with a single shot framing the bed perfectly and going on for over an hour. It started with the slow stripping of clothes. Then Aki said his name... his first name. It hadn't sounded better coming from anyone else's mouth before. Not Saehyun's. Not even Shinya's.

Then Aki's desperate pleas for Shinji to stop prepping and fuck him hard had woken Nao from his thoughts. Still Nao watched it all, wondering if Aki would say it again.

Nao swallowed.

How many times had he ended up replaying that moment? Even thinking about it got him hard again. He pushed the images aside.

Aki had better be ready for Nao as soon as he opened the door, or else they'd be having a serious talk about his future with the Matsukawa.

Nao opened the door to the warehouse. All the Russians crowded around the sofa stood. He stepped closer to the cluster, and a few of them moved to cover Ivan. Yet it was unavoidable; his pale skin glowed, popping each of his bulging blood vessels. He was dying and wouldn't last long.

"Here." Nao pushed the soup into the hands of the bow-tie Russian.

"Poison," he grunted out and shoved the soup back to Nao.

Nao refused to take it back, and the soup fell to the floor, the lid popping off. The plum fabric darkened. Too bad, because Yori had made some tasty soup. Would it be able to cure the Russian scum? No, but it was good nonetheless.

The air thickened, and Bow Tie stepped closer until he stood nose to nose with Nao. The Russian's breath stank more than Yori's dogs, but Nao didn't back down.

"We stand by what we said," Bow Tie said. "If Ivan dies, all are dead."

Nao laughed. "I'd like to see you try."

"Yeah?"

Nao pressed his forehead into the other and glared at him. "Maybe who I am hasn't made its way to your iceberg of a country, but I'm Nao fucking Murata of the Matsukawa. I single-handedly drove the Korean mob from Kyoto. You think I can't handle seven of you guys?"

Ivan gasped, reached out, and tugged on Bow Tie's hand. He said something in Russian, and Bow Tie's mouth dropped.

"Murata?" he whispered.

Nao grinned and crossed his arms. Finally, they were making progress. No thanks to Shinji and his translating ability. He should've explained who Nao was from the beginning, and the Russians wouldn't have had to worry about their leader dying.

"Do you have something new to say to me?" Nao asked.

Ivan said something more to Bow Tie, clutching onto his hand, but Bow Tie pulled it away.

"Nothing new," he said.

Nao grinned. "The moment you go up against my men is the moment you sign your death sentence."

Kohta clapped from the corner, and Nao rubbed his head. The blond could be such an idiot sometimes. Maybe Nao should've sent Kohta to work in one of the Matsukawa factions until he learned more tact. Either way, too much time had passed.

Nao went to him. "And how long were you just standing there? You're my bodyguard."

"I would've gotten in the way. I know when to step in." Kohta shrugged. "It's not like you can't hold your own against all these guys."

It was true, but still. Nao shook his head and pushed Kohta down the nearby hall.

"Where's Aki?" Nao asked.

"Probably resting."

Nao's eyes narrowed. "He's supposed to be working, not sleeping after Shinji fucks him."

"It's not that." Kohta shook his head. "I mean yeah, they totally did the old in-out, but Aki almost died last night."

Nao's eyes widened. "What? Those Russian bastards. I'll—"

Kohta grabbed hold of Nao's shoulder before he could run off.

"It wasn't the Russians," Kohta said. "He got lost in the snow for most of the night."

"Why would he do something stupid like that?"

"I don't know. Shinji said he ran out after you scolded him. Then the snowstorm hit, and he got lost."

Nao blinked until the words burned into him like boiling water thrown on his face. Aki had almost died because of him—because he didn't like the idea of Aki sleeping with anyone. What was Aki supposed to do, remain celibate for the rest of his life? Nao bit his cheek. His misguided jealousy hurt Aki more than Nao's pretending not to care. Nao had cared all along; that was why when Shinji first showed any signs of attraction toward Aki, Nao hated him.

Nao closed his eyes. He had to let Aki go and not just tell himself he didn't care anymore. He had to mean it. If he cared about Aki even half as much as his heart screamed when seeing him with Shinji, he'd know it was better to allow Aki the happiness he could never share with Nao.

Nao covered his mouth then swept his fingers up to rub the water out of his eyes. "Is Aki okay now?"

Kohta laughed and winked. "From what I heard this morning, Shinji took real good care of him."

Nao wanted to gag but laughed along with Kohta. "That's good. Aki should be back to normal soon."

"Maybe with a bit of a limp."

The words rubbed Nao raw, but he let it pass. He had to. He needed to let Aki go.

Nao cleared his throat. "Speaking of pain. Out of all the places yakuza get tattoos, you got a dragon on your dick?"

Kohta rubbed the back of his head and laughed. "He got the movie uploaded already? Damn, Shinji's good if he can edit it so quickly. I think Shinji's got the right idea, being surrounded by ladies all the time."

"He seems to be okay with men, too," Nao said.

Kohta laughed. "The best of both worlds, huh? You liked my

video, then? You think I'm good enough to maybe do a few more back home? We got a film studio."

"They do period movies, not porn."

"But they have the equipment. Maybe you can talk about it with Sakai. Porn is a solid investment."

Nao crossed his arms. "The only reason you got enough time here to act with your dick is because most of the time, I'm at Yori's house. In Kyoto, you're my guard full time."

"See, that's what I'm saying. Back home, I have no time to meet the ladies."

Nao rubbed his temple. Kohta might've looked like Shinya, but every time he opened his mouth and spoke, the illusion shattered. Maybe he could insist Kohta not be allowed to speak when he was around. It would probably be an impossible request.

"You still weren't able to get any guns?" Nao asked, changing the subject.

Kohta kicked his foot against the ground, knowing better than to bring up the budding porn industry Kyoto could offer any longer.

"Nah, I searched all over, and the only guns are the ones the Russians have. Maybe the guys didn't want the ladies accidently getting hold of one or something." Kohta shrugged. "I took the kitchen knives, so we've got something."

"Ivan looks like he won't make it through the night." Nao pressed his lips together. "I have a plan to get you two armed, but I need Aki. When he gets up, tell him to meet me at Yori's place."

"You want me to get him now? I think Shinji's with him now."

"Yea—" Nao stopped himself from allowing jealousy to sink in. Almost dying deserved some rest.

"No," Nao said. "Aki needs his rest, too. You can walk him up there if he thinks he needs it, but he needs to come to the door alone, got it?"

Kohta held up his thumb. "Got it, Boss."

CHAPTER 26

· · ·

FOR ONCE AKI'S hands weren't paper white; instead they were a
blistering red, and each of his fingertips was a waxy wooden
nub. After Shinji warned him up, Aki had enough sense to take
off his contacts before sleeping. He slipped on his black-framed
glasses and dressed in one of his fresher suits. Each buttonhole
took twice as long as each tiny movement of his hands were
like clumsy blocks.

He left his bedroom and strolled into the living room. Usually
the room was crowded with both the Russian taking care of
Ivan and a set of Mafufugumi playing cards as they waited for
their turn to be filmed. But the only people there were Kohta
and Shinji and a big bloodstain on the sofa where Ivan usually
rested.

"Did the Russians leave?" Aki asked.

Kohta laughed. "Wishful thinking there."

Shinji pulled out a chair for Aki. "They wanted to take Ivan to one of their rooms."

Aki nodded. That wasn't good. Even if Ivan wasn't really dead, the Russians could still attack them and no longer have the vailed excuse that they were waiting.

"I know what you're thinking, and if they wanted to do it, they would've attacked you guys already," Shinji said. "They're not as bad as you guys keep making them out to be."

"Well, you can understand why we disagree." Kohta glanced toward Aki. "You feeling better?"

"Better." Aki flexed his fingers and grimaced. "Are there any bandages?"

"Oh, babe, your hands are raw," Shinji said.

Kohta winked. "I'm sure that's not the only part of him that's raw."

Aki's cheeks heated, which only made Kohta laugh. Sure, when Aki was younger, he'd treated sex as casually as Kohta, but once Aki had joined the family, he'd slowed down and realized the need to foster relationships built on mutual respect.

"Hey, you should be happy. You almost died out there," Kohta said. "What did Nao end up saying to you?"

"He didn't want me to make his tea anymore."

Even saying it out loud left a bitter taste in Aki's mouth like leaves left to steep too long. Kohta's snickering turned into a full-out laugh. Shinji eyed him and took out a first aid kit from underneath the kitchen sink. He wrapped the gauze around Aki's fingers.

Aki slowly shook his head, trying to recall what exactly had happened in the snow. Yet everything grew so blank, like he'd been one of the snowflakes trapped in the storm.

"I started hallucinating out there." Aki tugged on his ear, which stung just as much as his hands when he touched them.

"Hypothermia makes people do funny things," Shinji said.

"I chatted with my dead grandfather over ramen, and I swear there was a naked girl in the snow."

Kohta laughed. "Instead of sirens calling you to sea, you had a naked girl drawing you deeper into the snow."

"She was like ten."

"Ew, Aki, you're a perv."

"That's disgusting. She wasn't naked in a horrifying way. Looking back on it now, of course some foreign girl wouldn't be in the snow."

Shinji's fingers tickled Aki's palm. "Well, I'm glad I managed to find you. Did you go straight to the train station?"

Aki pulled back his bandaged hand and flexed his fingers. It hurt a little less, but he'd probably take some painkillers once Shinji finished his other hand.

"I was completely lost before I found the train station." Aki pushed up his glasses. "I was following the phone signals, hoping to get to call Kurosawa."

"Any luck?" Kohta asked.

Aki shook his head. "Something else Father Murata can add to my list of disappointments."

Kohta moved his hand to ruffle Aki's hair, but he slapped

it away. He could be so irritating. Aki narrowed his eyes and stared at Kohta's half-unbuttoned dress shirt. It was a neon green-and-red boa pattern.

"How do you still have new clothes?" Aki said. "It was supposed to be a weekend trip."

"I packed extra. You never know where we could've ended up, and I wanted to be dressed for every occasion."

"How many pairs of shoes did you bring?"

Kohta rocked back in his chair. "Why do you want to know?"

Shinji laughed. "Are you a shoe collector?"

"If he had his way, all the shoe cubbies at headquarters would be dedicated to his shoes," Aki said.

"I dated ladies like that before," Shinji said.

"Come on, how many did you bring? Four? Five?"

Kohta mumbled something.

"What was that?" Aki held his hand to his ear. "Twenty-five pairs?"

"I said seven. I'm not that bad."

Shinji and Aki laughed, with Aki sharing the top ten of Kohta's worst clothing items. The conversation and jokes between the trio flowed easily while Shinji finished bandaging up Aki's hand.

"Once the boss gets his second bodyguard, I'm out of that tiny shared room at headquarters and into my own place."

"Don't tell me you're gonna get a two-bedroom place so all your garish designer clothes can have their own room." Aki laughed.

"Then I'll finally be living the yakuza dream."

"The yakuza dream?"

Kohta crossed his arms. "Come on, everyone wants the dream. Getting tons of money and all the ladies. Maybe you just want all the men and paper you can get."

"Is that all you think I care about, men and paper?"

Kohta shrugged. "That's all you let me know about you. You feeling back to normal now?"

"Yeah." Aki flexed his fingers. They stung a little, but nothing more.

"Then Boss wants to see you."

"Father Murata was here? But he usually doesn't show up until the afternoon."

Kohta shrugged. "He came early with soup."

"Why didn't you get me?"

"Because you almost died in the snow. Boss said to meet him at Yori's place when you get up."

"I should go now, then."

"Do you need help getting there?" Shinji asked.

Nao would kill him if he strolled up with Shinji.

Aki shook his head. "I know the way."

"Okay, babe, just be careful." Shinji pecked Aki on the cheek.

Aki crossed his arms. "He's my boss. I'll be fine."

"I meant in the snow. What did you think I meant?"

"Oh." Aki pressed his lips together. "Sorry."

"Just be safe."

Aki grabbed his coat and walked out. Yet as he climbed the mountain, the anger in Nao's face as he poured out the tea flowed over and over in Aki's mind. If he wasn't making Nao's tea, then it reduced his job just to answering his phone, and anyone could do that.

Aki's breath caught in his throat. He stopped, and the white snow almost enveloped him. Maybe the reason Nao hadn't cared that he wasn't ready at the door was because he was going to fire him. It would've been the second time in two days Aki wasn't ready for Nao.

Aki took off his glasses and rubbed the tears out of his eyes. It was not his place to change Nao's mind. He was their godfather, and Aki swore allegiance to him and the family over sake each year. There was nothing he could do but accept his fate.

CHAPTER 27

• • •

AKI'S SHOULDERS TENSED as he knocked on Yori's front door. He rubbed his gloved hand over his face after a few seconds passed, and no one answered the door.

Had Nao heard?

Should he knock again?

He held up his hand but then swallowed.

Why should he want to get fired more quickly? As long as he stayed outside, he'd remain Nao's secretary.

Aki's chest tightened, and he closed his eyes.

That's right. He might've pissed Nao off enough to no longer make tea, but Nao couldn't be ready to fire him.

"What are you doing here?"

Aki opened his eyes, and Yori stood with her arms folded over her chest, her stare colder than the air.

"I—ah." Aki rubbed the back of his neck.

"Watanabe warned you guys what would happen if you came up here and disturbed me."

"You see, Father Murata asked me."

She tapped her foot. "Did he now? He knows Watanabe doesn't like competition."

"Watanabe won't have to worry about that with me."

"Aki!" Nao called.

Hearing Nao call him by his first name robbed Aki of his senses, but then Nao wrapped his arms around him. Aki's eyes widened before he melted into Nao and returned the embrace. Aki's knees wobbled, but it only made Nao squeeze him tighter.

Then Nao pulled back. Aki knew it couldn't last forever, but inside, Aki screamed for more.

"I'm so happy you're safe," Nao said.

"I humbly apologize—"

Nao leaned forward and kissed Aki, completely cutting off his words and his thoughts. Aki's heart fluttered in his chest. Then Nao's tongue slid against his lips, begging Aki to allowed him entry. He opened, and his whole mouth became filled with Nao.

Aki had to be hallucinating.

He had to be still trapped in the snow.

Or maybe he'd died and gone to heaven.

Either way, Nao deepened the kiss, bringing his hands to cup Aki's face and positioning him to get a better angle. Aki trembled underneath Nao's push for dominance, maneuvering his tongue wherever Nao desired it.

Aki had dreamed about even the simplest kiss, but even his wildest fantasy hadn't matched this intensity. Nao tasted like the sweetest tea, and Aki would let Nao devour him.

The kiss was sloppy, almost animalistic, and it went straight to Aki's cock.

Yori cleared her throat. "Excuse me."

Nao pulled away, his cheeks red. His hand fell into Aki's and gave it a squeeze. Aki was too caught up in the high to even register the dull sting.

"Aki almost died yesterday." Nao looked down for a second before looking back at Yori. "He got lost in the snow, and I was so worried when I heard and...I...I..."

"You almost died?" she repeated.

Aki nodded and took off one of the gloves to show his bandaged hand. "I lost consciousness. They found me on the bench by the train station."

"You poor thing." Yori covered her mouth. "Even your ears are raw."

"I wanted to see him someplace more private." Nao dug a small hole into the snow with his socked foot. "I hope you can understand now why I asked him to meet me here."

She cracked a smile. "It's clear Watanabe doesn't have to worry about this one charming me. You two probably want your privacy."

"Aki sometimes can't hold himself back." Nao chuckled and squeezed Aki's shoulder. "Sometimes at headquarters he's so loud, everyone knows what we're up to."

Aki blinked.

The only time they were ever together at headquarters had been fake. A bitter smile crossed Aki's face as his heart tore itself into bits.

It was all fake.

"You two can wait until we're out of earshot, yeah?" She winked.

Nao smiled and patted Aki's hand. "I think we can manage."

Aki didn't know which hurt worse: the pulsing pain from the frostbite or the lies Nao spoke so easily. Nao played with his feelings so easily. Didn't he have even the smallest amount of empathy?

They said nothing as Nao tugged Aki into the house. He even helped Aki with his shoes and coat like a lover would. They sat on the sofa, with Nao pulling Aki close and wrapping his arms around him. Aki's body tensed, and he ignored the sweet nothings Nao whispered into his ear.

It was all a lie.

A show for Yori.

He was just a prop for whatever Nao wanted at the time. Aki took off his glasses and rubbed between his eyes. He sighed. He should've known better. Nao would never care about Aki's feelings when he had the city to take care of.

Aki's tongue grew heavy in his mouth, and a sour taste filled it. Then Aki caught a glimpse of the burn in on Nao's wrist. It had to be from Miko, since Nao had quit smoking ages ago. The meeting between then must've not run as smoothly as Nao had made it seem. It was silly to think Nao's biggest worried was Aki's relationship with Shinji or his feelings. Nao had to carry the will of Kyoto and the good for all the Matsukawa on his shoulders.

Yori walked into the living room, surrounded by a pack of dogs and children.

"You two enjoy yourselves," Yori said.

Nao smiled. "Thanks for this."

It took Yori forever to get everyone out the door.

She shut the door, but Nao clutched onto Aki for an eternity. Aki curled his fingers into a fist, ignoring the pain, and dug his knuckles into his leg.

Eventually, Nao stood and checked then pushed down the blinds in the window.

"I needed your help, and that was the only way to get her out of here." He couldn't even bother looking at Aki.

"Whatever I can do to please you brings me happiness." Even when he was angry, he couldn't escape the habit of laying his Kyoto dialect on thick for Nao.

"She has something in her room. The two of us together should be able to search through it before she gets back."

Nao grabbed something from a drawer then ran his fingers through his hair. "Look, I'm glad you made it out fine."

"Sure."

"The kiss was the only way to get her out of the house. What I had to do was absolutely necessary—"

"I said I understand," Aki cut in.

Nao turned around. "You and Shinji are hitting it off well."

Aki opened his mouth then closed it. "He's nice."

"Be careful he doesn't confuse you for one of his prostitutes."

"He wouldn't do that."

"Really?" Nao crossed his arms. "Why else do you think Shinji records you?"

Aki's cheeks grew hot. How had Nao known that Shinji had recorded the times they were together?

"I don't know what you're talking about."

"You should see the comments underneath your debut in porn. How they can't get enough of the two-toned freak."

Aki narrowed his eyes. "What?"

Nao shook his head. "Let's get moving. There's no telling when she'll come back."

"Which one is her door?"

"This way."

Aki pushed past Nao and to the door. Nao used the butter knife to turn the lock and open it. He clicked on the light. Aki rubbed his arms as a chill shot through him.

"Is it colder in here, or is it just me?" Aki asked.

"It's strange."

"What exactly are we looking for?"

"I don't know." Nao opened one of the nightstand drawers and rummaged through it. "She's keeping something in here hidden."

Everything appeared normal. She'd somehow even made her bed. With so many children, Aki thought she wouldn't have time. There was a bowl of half-forgotten soup left out on the nightstand, but that wasn't odd. The furniture looked a little big for the space, with the bed and nightstand taking up most of the room. On the other side was a desk with a laptop on it and a dresser. Two doors flanked the objects.

"Keep looking. Something's in here she doesn't want found."

Aki swallowed and watched Nao for a second before returning to his own search. Nao wouldn't have known about the videos unless Shinji had uploaded them on the website and Nao found them. He must've been mistaken. He'd told Shinji to delete the video, and he had.

Aki opened one of the doors in the bedroom, which led to the bathroom. He opened the drawers there, but unless she didn't want Nao to know exactly how many different types of bubble bath she owned, she had nothing.

"Wait. There isn't a fireplace," Nao said.

Aki left the room. "Was there supposed to be one?"

"She made a huge deal about how Watanabe built one for her."

"Maybe she's just trying to make herself seem more important to Watanabe."

Nao shook his head. "No. She has a huge pile of firewood outside. If she didn't have a fireplace, why would she bother?"

"Maybe she's selling it? Shinji seemed worried about the Mafufugumi finances."

"But she had enough for three winters. The point would be to sell it, not hoard it." Nao rubbed his temple. "Just keep looking."

Aki nodded and looked under the bed while Nao dug through more of the drawers. They searched in silence for a few minutes, but then Nao cleared his throat.

"Did you find something?" Aki asked.

Nao looked away. "I don't care what you do in your free time as long as it doesn't interfere with your work. Come on, we only have a few minutes before she gets back."

Aki swallowed back his protest and opened the other door. It led to a nice walk-in closet. Good. He could bury himself underneath all of Yori's clothes.

Shinji wouldn't post the videos of them online. It was just some kinky thing he was into. He especially wouldn't do it after Aki had asked him to delete the first one. Aki shook his head. Nao must've gotten him confused with someone else with vitiligo.

Aki pushed back the hanging clothes, revealing a pile of dirty laundry. He'd bring up the videos with Shinji when he got back. There was no reason to jump to conclusions.

Aki tried to push the pile of clothes back, but it was too heavy. He narrowed his eyes and grabbed at a few of the garments.

His mouth fell open. Underneath the first layer of clothes was a corpse.

"Nao!" Aki yelled, completely forgetting all formality.

Nao ran over, and Aki gulped. It was a little girl. The underside of her arm looked burnt, and the fingers on both her hands were black.

Aki's hand shook. "I thought I was hallucinating, but I saw another foreign girl out in the snow. They look the same age."

"This is who Yori was hiding."

"But why would she hide a little girl?"

Barking dogs drew closer, and Nao ran out of the room.

CHAPTER 28

• • •

NAO'S NERVES IGNITED as he ran out of the room. Yori would have to explain every last detail she had been hiding from him. Nao met her in the living room as she opened the door. The dogs swept in, barking and jumping up on Nao, but he ignored them.

"I hope you two enjoyed your time together," Yori said, helping one of her kids out of her coat.

"What was the fireplace Watanabe build for you made of?" Nao asked.

"Stone."

Nao brushed past Yori and stood outside.

He crossed his arms and glanced at the roof. "Funny, I don't see any chimney here."

"It's a new construction type. Only needs a pipe."

Nao narrowed his eyes and glared at Yori. Aki stood behind her so she was trapped. There was no way she could run away from his questions.

"We went into your bedroom and saw no sign of a fireplace."

"How dare you enter my—"

Nao took a step closer and stood strong. "There was a dead girl in your closet."

Yori took a step back, pushing her children behind her.

"What were you chopping all that wood for? You don't have a fireplace, so you don't need it."

She looked away. There had to be something about the wood stack he was missing. Nao stood centimeters from her but remained silent. She was better than most men.

"Fine, if you're not going to answer, I'm going to have to get to the bottom of this myself."

Nao raced toward the back of the house. The firewood stack dominated the snow. The logs weren't stacked in rows on top of one another but around something.

Aki was behind her, pushing her whenever she shuffled to a stop. Nao's nostrils flared. What was she hiding? Slowly she emerged from the corner, dragged her feet in the snow.

"Are you going to tell me what's inside, or am I going to have to look myself?" Nao yelled over the howling wind.

"Please, don't," she pleaded.

She ran toward Nao, but Aki grabbed her coat collar and held her in place.

"Do what he says," Aki warned.

Yori cried out more supplications. He wasn't going to get an answer from her.

Nao push on the side of the stack, and the wood tumbled down to reveal another dead child. He pushed more of the stack over. His lips dried in the swirling air as his mouth dropped open.

Five dead children.

Four girls and one boy.

Their fingers were black, and most of their bodies were curled and contorted in odd positions. They were clothed, but not in coats or jackets. It was like they had been plucked from the inside of a house and put in the log coffin.

Aki gasped, and Yori fell to her knees.

Nao pointed. "Why are you collecting dead children?"

Tears rolled from her eyes.

"Speak!"

Aki pressed a hand on Yori's shoulder. "It's okay. We just want to know what's going on."

She sniffed as the dogs played around in the snow. Giichi must've locked the younger children inside, because none of them were there. He was a smart kid.

"Don't tell Watanabe," she begged.

Nao crossed his arms. "Start talking and we'll see."

She took in a deep breath and rubbed her eyes. "It started when we all went down to the shore for the summer. Shinji was there to take a family video."

"What does this have to do with the dead children in your yard?"

She bit her bottom lip then continued. "He put up a video of my daughters on that site. They were just playing on the beach, nothing more. But then so many perverts commented on how they wanted more."

Nao grimaced. "Why would Shinji take such a risk putting Watanabe's daughter up for kiddy porn?"

She swallowed and shook her head. "Watanabe made some

bad investments, and money is tight. He's not saying it, but I know. When he used to visit, he'd bring something for all the kids, but he hasn't done that in years."

Nao nodded. Something had been off, with all the buildings the Mafufugumi owned. No wonder they hadn't gotten Jun out of the jail the first night. They hadn't had enough money to bribe the police.

"So, these kids were meant to be in Shinji's videos?" Nao asked.

She rubbed her eyes with the back of her arm. "The Russians loaned Shinji ten kids two weeks ago. He was supposed to pay from the profits the first few weeks of videos earned. Children? Can you believe it?"

Nao shook his head. "How did they end up dead?"

"When I came down to teach the ladies Japanese like I do with all of them, I saw them. How could I not see my own children's faces in theirs after that? I couldn't allow them to be violated and then sold off, but I couldn't ask Watanabe to let them go. I'm not supposed to go down there, and Shinji said the children were the thing to turn the Mafufugumi's money problems around."

Aki's jaw dropped, the color draining from his face as his eyes bulged out. He stumbled back but caught himself from falling.

It was tragic, but at least he had some more leverage over the Mafufugumi. They needed the Matsukawa's monthly payments to keep above water. So they were as desperate for the alliance as they were, since sealing it would bring a monthly sum for the Mafufugumi's services.

"How did one end up in your house?" Aki asked.

She rubbed her eyes. "I tried to save them. I told one that I lived on top of the hill and that I would think of a plan to save them. But they tried to escape by themselves. One of them set a fire, and while Shinji was distracted, she let the others out. It was dark, and only one of them made it to my house alive."

"You tried to nurse her back to health while I was there," Nao said.

Yori nodded. "She died last night, but I couldn't take her out without you noticing, so I left her in my closet. I've been going out trying to find the other children to give them a proper funeral. I want to get to them before anyone else can."

Aki gasped. "I found one last night. I don't remember where, though, but they're out there."

She shook her head. "He lost so much money on this deal. Please don't tell him I'm the reason for it. I should've called the police and ratted the whole thing out, but he's the father of my children and there's no way I can leave him."

Nao laughed and crossed his arms. "He didn't lose any money since he made the Matsukawa pay for the mistake."

Tears ran down her cheeks. "Please don't tell him the truth. I have a baby on the way and—"

"Then I won't tell him, but only if you give my men guns and ammo. The Russians want to start stuff with us. I'm not going to let my men be at a disadvantage. Watanabe wouldn't leave you here alone without access to that safe."

Yori bowed. "Of course. Anything you need."

"The internet, too," Aki added. "I need to get in contact with home."

Nao raised a brow. "Shinji wouldn't let you do it?"

"Not during his uploads.

"Hmmm, sounds like there are more things you need to discuss with him."

"There are a lot of answers I want from Shinji now, but keeping contact with him is my priority."

Nao smiled. "Good to know you put the family first."

CHAPTER 29

· · ·

AKI HAD NEVER carried a gun for so long in his life. Sure, he'd practiced with Nao and Kohta, but because of the strict gun laws, Nao had forbidden Aki from keeping one on him daily.

All throughout the trek from Yori's home to the warehouse, the wind howled in Aki's ear. The guns tucked into his waistband grew as cold as icicles. The sun lowered, bathing the snow in golden light, but no amount of tugging at his coat blocked the cold, and his steps became more rushed halfway down the hill. At least everything back home was quiet.

He locked his gaze on the warehouse, almost afraid if he blinked it would disappear. His hurried steps made him sink deeper in the snow, dumping more of it into his shoes and soaking the bottom of his pants.

On the way up, the trip hadn't felt so frigid, but on that journey, his heart had guided him. It had radiated throughout his body and warmed each snowflake until it was nothing but a

glittering jewel. But Aki's heart had hardened on the trip down. It turned the snow around him into nothing but a chilling reminder of Nao's icy affection toward him and Shinji's betrayal of his trust.

Aki opened the door to the warehouse, and stale air filled his nose even though it was almost dinnertime, and someone should've been cooking. Aki swallowed and opened his jacket. The room wasn't wrecked, so maybe nothing had happened. The Russians could've simply killed Kohta in a different room. But then they would've shot Aki the moment he stepped through the door.

Aki blew out a few short breaths and listened. Nothing came but the whistling of the wind against the metal roof. Aki pulled one of the guns forward. His coat would still hide the weapon, but he'd have easier access to it should he need it. With his hands at the ready for a quick draw, he crept his way behind the sofa.

No one.

That made one room clear.

Maybe Kohta had done the smart thing and barricaded himself in his room.

Aki's attention darted between the two hallways on opposite ends as he skirted the room to Kohta's. Aki put one hand on the doorknob and gave one final glance toward the opposite hall. He used his body to block the sight of the weapon and turned the knob.

"It's me," he said, allowing the door to swing itself open as he took cover.

No ring of bullets came, nor a word from Kohta. With as much talking as he did, he was either dead on the bed or wasn't there. Aki cautiously approached, checking behind the door and the closet for any hidden Russians.

No one was there, but the room was a fucking mess. Kohta's brightly colored clothes were strewn about the room. They put on a better light show than the last gay dance club Aki had visited. He could add slob to the long list of why Kohta wasn't fit to be by Nao's side.

Aki sighed. Even after Nao had stomped on his heart, Aki was still jealous of the relationship Nao had with Kohta. Aki couldn't help it, though. The immense power Nao possessed drew Aki in like tea leaves to water. No matter how Aki wanted to get away, his very being yearned to be enveloped by him. Aki hugged his elbows. He needed to survive the Russians if he wanted to see Nao again. Even when he'd screwed Shinji, he thought of Nao.

Aki left Kohta's room and took the same precautions, checking his room and the others down that hall. When they all turned up empty, he went back to the living room and to the door leading to the studio. Kohta could've been filming another porn with Shinji.

Acid built up in Aki's throat, and he swallowed it down. Even thinking of Shinji sent chills down Aki's spine.

No one in their right mind would want to film child porn. Aki could almost understand it if Watanabe had threatened Shinji with a bullet if he hadn't produced the movies, but Yori said Shinji suggested it, even going so far as to put Watanabe's own daughter up on display in a bid for him seeing the profits and wanting more.

It was disgusting.

Uploading the videos of the times Shinji and Aki were together was nothing in comparison. He shook his head. How could he ever have fallen for someone like that?

He turned the knob on the studio door, but it was locked. Aki groaned. Shinji must've decided to keep it locked after Nao had barged down there.

"Fucking hell!" Kohta screamed.

With his hand on his gun, Aki dashed toward the sound of Kohta's voice. He knew whatever was going on couldn't be good. His heart pounded in his chest, but then as he drew closer, he heard laughter.

"Shit, man, that's a month's pay."

"You guys up for another round?" Kohta said.

Aki pushed the gun into the back of his waistband and shook out the tingling in his arms. Light poured out of one of the bedrooms as Aki stood in the doorway. Kohta and three of the Mafufugumi were playing poker. Aki shook his head. They must not have learned their lesson from before.

"We should play something else." One Mafufugumi member elbowed the other. "Kohta keeps kicking our asses."

Kohta shuffled the cards. "Whatever you guys want, but pick something already."

"Maybe we should stop."

"Nah, come on. Shinji locked up all the girls. We got nothing else to kill time with."

Aki cleared his throat, getting all of their attention. "Hey, Kohta, I need to chat with you."

Kohta shrugged. "Nothing's stopping you."

"I'm sure Father Murata would want our conversation to be private."

Kohta stood. "I guess I'll give you guys a round to regain your confidence."

Kohta left the room, and Aki pulled him into the nearby room.

"What did the boss want?" Kohta asked.

Aki pulled out one of the guns and handed it to Kohta. "He got us weapons."

"Awesome." Kohta shoved the gun in the back of his waistband. "You gonna be okay with this? Ivan has as much chance of making it through the night as these guys have of beating me tonight."

Aki laughed. "Father Murata has taken us both for practice shooting."

"Yeah, but I always hit more targets than you."

Aki shook his head. "I'll be ready if the Russians attack."

"Okay, just be on your toes. The Mafu-peeps aren't going to help us at all with this."

"Because they're cowards at the hands of foreigners."

Kohta laughed. "You sound like the boss now."

"Yeah, well, I like hanging around him. So, I'm going to survive."

"What happened?"

"What do you mean?"

"Your mood's all off. If Boss said something, then you'd be happy to be here, but you look too pissed. Trouble in paradise with you and Shinji?"

"Shinji suggested, filmed, and uploaded kiddy porn."

Kohta grimaced. "Sick."

"Yeah."

"And here I thought it was because you said Nao's name when you two were fucking."

Aki narrowed his eyes. "How did you know that?"

"I took a guess. Figured I had a fifty-fifty with it being right, and it's you, so my odds were probably better."

"You're an ass."

Kohta snickered. "Whenever you and Boss start fucking, this job will finally be as peaceful as a trip to the outlet stores."

"Don't be so obscene."

"You both want it. Maybe we should find a way for you two to get locked in an elevator like they do in TV shows. Then Nao will see what he's missing without being with you."

A shiver ran down Aki's spine, and the pieces clicked into place. He'd stooped to the lowest of the low by fucking Shinji. It would be impossible for Nao to look at him the same way. If he even had a sliver of a chance with Nao, it had vanished. Aki sighed. He needed to give up already.

"Are you really playing cards at a time like this?" Aki asked.

"We're right beside where the Russians keep Ivan."

Aki shook his head. "Just between us, I think he's already dead. They're probably just waiting for the right moment to attack."

"Well, then it's good we got these nice shiny guns, and it would be better to stay in a crowd," Kohta said.

"Safety in numbers?"

"You bet your ass. You going to join me, then?"

Aki narrowed his eyes. "No more cheating."

Kohta laughed. "I wasn't cheating."

"Yeah, and Father Murata made out with me."

"Come on, I won't cheat you. Boss will be happy that I'm getting some of the money back he paid for those girls."

"But it's going in your pocket, not the Matsukawa coffers."

Kohta shook his head. "Let's just play cards."

CHAPTER 30

◆ ◆ ◆

HOURS PASSED, AND if Aki could stay up another three hours, he'd be able to hear the train coming... if it was coming. Shinji had kept himself locked up in the basement. He probably knew Ivan was dead and didn't want to get involved with the aftermath. He was such a disgusting coward.

Aki rubbed his eyes and threw his cards down. "It's getting too late for this."

"Come on, one more round," one of the Mafufugumi said.

"Aren't you tired of losing money?"

"But how will I get it back if we don't keep on playing?"

Aki rolled his eyes. These Mafufugumi had to have some kind of gambling addiction.

"Maybe if we switched to mahjongg or hanafuda cards. These are making my eyes hurt."

The Mafufugumi laughed and elbowed the guy next to him. "Bozo here lost one of the mahjongg tiles the last time we recorded here."

"We had to throw so much stuff out because of that fire. How was I supposed to know Shinji used them for part of a set?"

Aki shook his head. "Whatever. I'm off to bed. You should get some sleep, too."

Kohta threw his head back. "Come on, Aki, you're good—"

A shuffle in the room beside them stopped Kohta in midsentence. He nodded at Aki and then threw the table on its side. Aki scrambled for cover while the Mafufugumi yelled about the money getting knocked over. They had no idea what was about to go down.

In a single second, Aki was wide awake. His breath came in shallow gasps as his muscles locked tight. Kohta and Aki sat back to back and pulled out their guns. Aki swallowed, hoping it would calm his twisting stomach. Until all the Russians were silenced, he wouldn't even think about sleeping again.

"You got this?" Kohta asked.

"I'll get the ones on the right and you the left?"

Kohta cocked the gun. "I'm ready."

The door slammed open, and shots were fired before Aki could react. His heart thumbed in his chest as the echo of each shot rang in his ears. Kohta fired his shots back with equal vigor.

One of the Russians cried out as he fell to the floor. Some of the Mafufugumi were also hit in the crossfire, but the rest cowered behind the table.

Aki held his breath and peeked out from the corner of the table and stared down the Russian with the split lip. Bullet whizzed by him and shattered pieces of the edge of the table.

"Hurry up and shoot." Kohta turned back and reloaded a clip in his gun.

Aki exhaled and pulled the trigger. The shot rang out, and the Russian fell, clutching his chest. Kohta stood and finished him off with a bullet to the skull.

"Good shot," Kohta said.

Aki stood. "There's still four more," Aki said.

"Some of them might've headed for Boss."

"Let's clear the warehouse first."

Aki nodded, and they swept the immediate hallway.

"You go right and I'll go left?" Kohta said.

"Yeah."

His heart pounded in his chest, but he tried to keep his breath steady, knowing he needed to keep it calm or else his thoughts would become just as erratic. Aki hugged the corner of the hallway, glancing back at Kohta as he slowly entered one of the rooms.

Aki cleared the room and made his way to the bedrooms. He opened Kohta's bedroom door and held back before checking the inside, clearing the room like Nao had taught him to do. All Aki needed was to remember Nao's training and he'd live. Aki's steady steps took him inside Kohta's bedroom.

The breath whooshed out of Aki as the arms of one of the Russians wrapped around his neck in a headlock. He stood a head taller than Aki and used his strength to lift Aki off his feet.

Aki panicked.

He kicked but couldn't get loose.

He tried to fire off the gun, but his muscles wouldn't listen.

He dug his fingernails into the Russian's arm, but it only pushed his arm deeper against his windpipe.

His vision blurred as the room drained of color.

He was fucked.

The gun slipped from his fingers as it grew too heavy.

Shit.

A gunshot rang out, and Aki blinked.

The Russian loosened his grip and slumped against Aki. He pushed the body to the side, and a red stain covered his back. The Russian's head twitched, and he groaned. Aki snatched his gun and fired a shot to the base of his head.

"You okay?" Kohta asked.

Kohta had saved him. Aki rubbed his throat. Maybe the blond wasn't such an idiot after all.

"Thanks for that," Aki said.

"I told you I got your back." Kohta squeezed Aki's shoulder.

"We should check out the other rooms."

"Maybe together this time. We can work as a team."

Aki nodded. "Yeah, as a team from now on."

CHAPTER 31

• • •

EVERY TIME NAO closed his eyes, he could taste Aki.

Nao shook his head and opened his eyes again. How could he allow himself to get so carried away? The plan had been to simply hold Aki's hand, and if that wasn't enough to prove their relationship to Yori, Nao would've kissed him on the cheek. He hadn't meant to get so intense and out of hand.

Yet when Nao had finally seen Aki, the light touch of Aki's gloved hand hadn't been enough to slow Nao's beating heart or dissolve his fingers aching for real touch.

Once he'd started the kiss, it had been impossible to stop. Nao had needed Aki to understand he'd dumped the perfectly made tea out in jealous anger.

He hadn't meant for Aki to run out in the snow.

Nor for him to wander in a panic to find shelter.

He hadn't meant to almost lose him…

They couldn't be together, but Nao wanted Aki to feel how

much he wished they could. That kiss was their last kiss, and it would be the last Nao would ever have.

Nao traced his lips with his fingers, then he turned over on his futon. He closed his eyes, but the image of Aki appeared, calling out his name in a haughty moan. Nao groaned. It might be easier to stay up the few remaining hours of night and catch the weather report to see if the tracks had been cleared.

One of the dogs barked. It was a small yip, so it had to be the Chihuahua. Nao hadn't bothered learning their names. It wasn't like they responded to him anyway.

But then one of the others barked before it turned into a whimper, and any veil of sleep fell away. Nao grabbed his gun from underneath his pillow. He loaded a bullet into the chamber as a shadow crossed the window.

A crooked smile appeared on Nao's face. The Russians had finally put their pathetic threats into action. A hysterical laugh shook his whole body as the images flashed of all the ways Nao could slay them. They'd awakened the devil inside and its thirst for dyeing the Hokkaido tundra red with their blood.

In the quiet night, the floorboards outside his room squeaked, and Nao quietly slipped to the other side of the door. He put his finger on the trigger, not bothering to secure the belt of his yukata.

The knob turned, and the light behind cast a long shadow on the floor. From the gap under the door, Nao saw that the person entering wore shoes. He grinned and aimed about midway up the door and fired.

The man grunted and fell to the floor into the room as the

hollow door splintered. The Russian clutched his stomach. Nao stepped from behind the door and shot him twice in the head. Blood sprayed up, spattering Nao's yukata, and pooled around the man's exploded head.

Cries echoed through the house.

The gunshot must've woken up the children, but their screams might help Nao to slip out undetected. Nao clutched his gun. It also meant the Russian could do the same.

Nao groaned and pulled the dead Russian all the way into the bedroom. Blood soaked through Nao's indigo yukata and stuck to his chest. It didn't matter, though. He planned to bathe in Russian blood before the dawn. Nao threw a sheet over the body. If he could fool the Russian's comrades into thinking it was him for a few seconds, it would benefit him.

His muscles tightened as he closed the bedroom door behind him. Footsteps barreled down the other side of the house, and Nao took in a breath.

They had guns.

He had to stay controlled.

Not everyone in the house was a target, and though he would be fine lying to Watanabe if one of his offspring got caught in the crosshairs, Nao wanted to avoid it.

With careful steps, he walked down the hallway and kept to the shadows just before the living room. A figure moved out of the kids' room and into Yori's bedroom. The form had three heads. So it must've been Yori snatching her daughters and taking them to safety. One followed behind her. It had to be Giichi.

The front door flung open, and one of the Russians stepped in. He turned to Yori, and Nao ducked behind the sofa, taking aim underneath the cover. The Russian's movements were frantic, and he swooped down and snatched Giichi in his arms.

Giichi screamed, but Yori had stopped. She ran into her bedroom and slammed the door shut. Smart.

"Is that you, Murata, hiding in the dark?" the Russian yelled, his bad Japanese hurting Nao's ears.

Giichi struggled in the man's arms, but no matter how much he kicked, the guy didn't let go. Giichi's brightly colored Mario pajamas contrasted with the Russian's black clothes. The little stars above Mario's head glowing in the dark were the only indication of where Giichi's body ended and the Russian's started, but the way the Russian held Giichi, it was impossible to shoot without putting the kid's life in danger.

Nao's hand hugged the wall, slowly climbing up until he could switch the light on.

"Come out like a man, Murata!"

Nao narrowed his eyes, and he grabbed the bottom of the sofa. He stood, knocking it over, using the distraction to throw off whatever aim the Russian had on him. Nao took his aim, even though it was right through Giichi as well, and stepped closer. A knife tattoo cut through the Russian's neck.

So it was that one. Nao almost hoped it was Mr. Bow Tie he'd get to slaughter next, but Knife Guy would work too.

"Stay back, or I'll shoot 'em!" he yelled.

His hand shook as he put the gun against Giichi's head. Nao grinned and stepped forward. The Russian staggered back. The soft cries of Yori behind the door pressed Nao on.

"I said stay back!"

Nao put his finger on the trigger. "Let the kid go."

Tears ran down Giichi's cheeks, but his gaze kept locked on Nao, his eyes begging Nao to do something. Nao gave a small nod and took a step closer.

"I'll shoot him. I swear! One more step and I'll do it..." He muttered something in Russian.

"You think I care about some fucking kid?"

Nao grinned. The Russian pulled his gun away from Giichi's head and fired at Nao. He ducked and fired two shots of his own.

Giichi let out an agonized groan.

Blood stained his face, and the glow-in-the-dark stars dimmed with blood.

The Russian dropped the gun, and his arms slacked around Giichi.

Nao ran over and put two bullets in the Russian's skull. One of his eye sockets was ripped open and motionless as he stared up at Nao. He looked away. His father would be proud.

Yori pushed Nao to the ground and scooped up Giichi.

"You're okay. Mommy's got you now," she cried out.

She rubbed the blood off Giichi's face.

"You didn't get hit?" Nao asked.

He shook his head, biting his lip to stop himself from crying more.

Nao let out a faint smile and secured his yukata with his fabric belt. Blood weighed it down, but there were still more who needed to die.

"Barricade the door behind me then get to safety," Nao said.

"I'll come get you when I've slaughtered all the Russians."

She nodded and told Giichi to go to the bedroom and hide under the bed with his sisters. Nao headed for the door with Yori following.

"Good luck," she said.

Nao laughed. "Believe me, I won't need it."

She locked the door behind him.

All of Nao's muscles tingled. He no longer had to be careful. He could finally unleash the rage inside. The snow silenced his shoeless steps. There was no way of knowing where the Russian had decided to take cover.

Nao hugged the exterior wall of the house as he made his way around. His whole body grew hotter with a frenzied fire with each step. He would kill them all, and he had every right to. Japan belonged to the Japanese, and even if Watanabe forgot that fact, Nao would happily remind the Russian what stepping foot into Japan meant.

A shot rang out in the desolate snow.

A miss.

Nao flew to the woodpile for cover as shots stung his ears. Nao held his breath, and the distinct sound of reloading a gun rang out in the silent night. He looked up, and the hot breath of someone came over the woodpile before dissipating into the night.

Nao grinned and pushed that section of the woodpile over. At least a hundred logs tumbled down, and the Russian let out an agonizing groan.

A grin stretched across Nao's face as his toes dug into the

snow. He stepped around the pile, ignoring the dead children, once again exposed within their funeral pyre.

The Russian lay underneath the stack. His head stuck out, and he pressed his arms up in an attempt to free himself.

"How dare you come here!" Nao yelled.

The man said something before pulling out a gun from under his crushed body. He pointed it up at Nao and fired, but nothing happened. The clip had never been replaced.

Nao grinned. "Bad luck, huh?"

If there were any other of them out there, they weren't making themselves known.

Nao laughed and stepped closer.

"Which one are you, anyway?"

Nao grabbed a fistful of the guy's hair and jerked his head up. All their faces looked so similar, the only way Nao could really tell them apart was the tattoos they wore.

Then the top of a bow tie on the guy's neck showed in the twilight.

"It's you," Nao hissed and slammed Bow Tie's head into the snow.

A quick bullet in the head was much too good after what the bastard had said to Aki. Nao put his gun away and strode toward the ax. He caught of a glimpse of the burn on his wrist, and he laughed. Miko wanted the demon inside of Nao, then he'd show her what he could do.

Nao's thoughts flushed red with all the glorious things he could do with an ax. He'd killed people with a sword before, but those were quick slashes. There and dead. An ax would be a lot messier and the screams a lot sweeter.

He carried the ax over his shoulder and stood before Bow Tie. He kept on trying to struggle free, but the weight of the wood was too much for him.

"Now, I've never chopped wood before, so this might end up being a little messy." Nao chuckled.

He aimed for Bow Tie's hand, and when he brought the ax down, it chopped two of his fingers off.

His bloodcurdling scream filled Nao with delight and the desire for more.

"Look, you could be an ex-yakuza with those fingers gone. Now let's try the rest of your hand."

The ax came up again, snapping the wrist and severing the hand. His screams were the sweetest justice Nao could taste.

With no other limbs sticking out but Bow Tie's head, it left Nao with few options. A slight sting of disappointment fluttered across his mind. The Russian pleas or curses were left unnoticed.

Nao pressed his foot on the top of the guy's head and examined it with the ax hovering above. He stepped back and swung the ax down. The sound of it slicing through the air. It completely missed the place in Bow Tie's head Nao was aiming at, but it did slice open Bowtie's ear.

More pleas and struggle.

Ah, if only he realized they just encouraged Nao.

The next swing landed in the center of Bow Tie's skull. Nao smiled. He knew he'd get the hang of it eventually. He pulled at the ax, but it was securely stuck.

Nao groaned and pushed on the guy's bloody head with his foot. Blood squashed between his toes, and tiny fragments of bone stuck to his foot. With enough pulling, the ax was free.

The Russian's shallow groans excited Nao more, but another slam to the head silenced them.

But Nao didn't stop.

He couldn't stop.

Each blow of the ax sent more blood and brain goo onto the snow. It soaked through Nao's yukata. Yet each one was more satisfying than the next, and the adrenaline pumping through Nao's muscles meant he could go until dawn.

Sadly, the Russian's body didn't hold up much longer. His skull had been cracked in so many pieces, no part stuck up for Nao to smash. More flecks of blood splattered around the snow than there were stars in the sky.

Nao slammed the ax down onto the mush. Nao panted and wiped the sweat from his brow with his arms.

Aki!

He was still at the warehouse with three Russians Nao had yet to slaughter.

He broke into a run.

Coming down off the high of the kill, Nao's thoughts crushed him with his lack of care. If he wanted to be a good godfather, he should've ended Bow Tie's life quickly and helped his men.

Nao stopped as a figure came out of the snow. It was too far away to make out any detail. He raised his gun.

"Nao!" Aki yelled.

An electric jolt struck through Nao, and his knees almost gave out in the thick snow. Aki had called him by his first name. It sounded better than it did in the video.

The early-morning dawn sent a buttery yellow on the flittering snow. Nao smiled. Aki was fine. Nao cursed himself for doubting. Aki had trained even more than Kohta had on shooting and made sure he kept up his sparring at the gym. He was a model yakuza.

Aki gave a formal bow once he was close enough. His eyes grew wide. "Are you all right, Father Murata?"

"What?" Nao smiled and glanced down at his blood-soaked yukata. "Oh, this isn't my blood. The Russians are no match for me. I got three."

Aki nodded. "Kohta and I took care of the other three. We had no help from the Mafufugumi."

"The cowards." Nao glanced back toward Yori's home. "I should probably help her clean up."

"Of course."

Nao turned away and headed back. Yet as the distance grew between them, even if it was only a few steps, Nao knew it had been so much more. Even if nothing could become of them, he still selfishly wanted Aki by his side. Nao stopped the snow crunching under his feet.

"Aki," Nao called out and turned away.

"Yes, Father Murata."

"I was thinking, the power had been off at the warehouse. It must've affected the water. So the water is to blame for your tea being off, not you."

Aki's mouth hung open.

"Once we get out of here, I'd enjoy it if you could make tea for me again."

"As you wish. I'm happy to fulfill anything you desire."

Aki's whole face lit up, and Nao's cheeks hurt from smiling.

They stood in silence as the sun grew higher in the sky. But then Aki's smile faded into a frown.

"There's something I need to tell you." Aki balled his bandaged fingers into a fist. "Kurosawa ordered me to lie to you, and even though I rejected it at first, I followed what he asked of me. Before we arrived at the village, three Korean mob members were found defiling a temple. Kurosawa asked me not to tell you since they were caught and handed over to the police. He didn't want you to rush the agreement just to get back. It was wrong of me to withhold that information from you."

"Damn right it was."

"Please—

Nao held up his hand, silencing Aki.

"But I have wronged you too." Nao bowed. "I shouldn't have kissed you. I should've asked if it was okay first."

There was so much more Nao wanted to say but never could.

Aki closed the short distance between them, a grin crossing his face. "You're my godfather. I've sworn allegiance to you. You're more than welcome to use my body whatever way you see fit."

"Still." Nao cleared his throat and took a step back. He couldn't trust himself to be so close to him. "It's probably good we weren't in Kyoto, or else the city would've misinterpreted the kiss and you'd be dead."

Aki tilted his head. "You can't really believe that?"

"The city has killed everyone I love."

"Couldn't there be a possibility that it might've been coincidence?"

Nao shook his head. "Impossible."

CHAPTER 32
• • •

THE WAREHOUSE DOOR shut behind Aki, and he smiled, leaning against it. For once, no tension thickened the air, and he could breathe deeply, knowing where he stood with Nao.

Aki's fingers trailed over his lips. He could almost feel Nao tracing them with his tongue, longing to deepen their kiss. There had been too much emotion behind their locked lips to be completely fake. Underneath Nao's failed logic, Aki felt a renewed chance to steal Nao's heart away from the city he loved. Why else would a man powerful enough to rise to the rank of godfather at twenty-six apologize to *his secretary* for not getting permission for a single kiss? No other man could come close to his feelings for Nao. His time with Shinji proved there was no point in even trying.

"What are you doing over there?" Kohta asked from the kitchenette.

"Nothing."

"The last girl I was with would always touch her lips like that, too."

"The weather's got them chapped."

"Here." Kohta reached into his pocket and pulled out a small tube. "You can borrow my lip balm."

He placed it on the surface beside him, and Aki sighed, walking over. The radio on the counter played a soft jazz song as Aki picked up the metal tube and tapped his finger along it. French writing was etched along the side.

Kohta rolled his eyes. "You're not going to catch anything if that's what you're worried about. The applicator is 24-karat gold, so it kills any bacteria."

Aki laughed. "Gold? But you're just going to throw it away when you're done."

"But it's the best one out there."

"Just because it's the most expensive doesn't mean it's the best."

"Give it a try, and then try to tell me it's not the best thing you've had on your lips."

Kohta crossed his arms while Aki took off the cap and dabbed some on his lips. It was smooth, and the light lemon scent was a refreshing break from the arctic weather. Still, Kohta had probably spent a day's income on such a tiny bottle. Though with as much money as Kohta won while playing poker, maybe to him it was pocket change.

"You like it, don't you?" Kohta nudged Aki with his elbow.

Aki shrugged, putting the tube back on the counter. "It's fine."

"Fine? You mean amazing."

"Should I say it changed my life?"

"It would help me feel better."

"Like your ego needs any more boosting."

Kohta snapped up the balm, dabbed some on his own lips, and let out a refreshed sigh like a lame commercial about mouthwash.

"Besides, when you pull this out, it gets all the ladies' attention," Kohta said. "They want to try it, and the next thing you know, you're checking into a love hotel with them."

"Can you only talk about women and brand names?"

"When I tried to talk about my new tattoo, you said to never bring it up again."

Aki rubbed his temple. "And you did it again. Every time I see a dragon, I still think of your dick. It's disgusting. Do you know how many dragons they have in Kyoto?"

Kohta smirked, and they both laughed. Kohta might not have been the most horrible person Nao could've made his bodyguard, but he was close. Talking about getting laid all the time and flashing how much money upper yakuza made were common. There were more than enough homophobic members of the family who would bite their tongue when it came to Nao but would lash out their hatred when they found Aki alone. Kohta, for all his flaws, never cared about Aki's sexuality or acted like it was contagious. Kohta had even taken Aki to a gay bar for his birthday, trying to get him laid since Nao clearly wasn't doing it. Maybe it was time to be friends, since they'd be stuck beside Nao so often.

"You know, if Boss would actually let me take a day off, I wouldn't talk about women half as much," Kohta said.

"Somehow I don't believe that." Aki crossed his arms. "Father

Murata's fine, by the way."

"I told you he would be."

"Still, you're his bodyguard. It's your duty to protect him."

"You tell him that. Half the time, Nao wants nothing more than being left alone so he can mope and think Kyoto is out to make him suffer."

Aki looked away. "That might be true."

"You know it is. He was probably happier you came to see if he was all right than if I'd trekked up that snowy hill."

"Maybe."

"Nao will see you've got the hots for him since day one." Kohta ruffled Aki's hair, but Aki swatted his hand away. "Don't worry. One day, you'll get his D."

"Don't call it that."

"Hey, you know what? Maybe since you've been doing the dirty with Shinji all trip, it will make Nao jealous and he'll realize his feelings for you."

Aki's hands briefly clenched, and he sighed out the lingering high of Nao's apology. Aki had delayed dealing with Shinji long enough. With the threat of a Russian putting a bullet in his skull gone, it was time to deal with it. Compartmentalizing each aspect of life was how Aki had learned to survive in the yakuza underworld. In the moments when aspects bled into each other, Aki's fingers would twitch, and he'd be reduced to a manic paper folder. His relationship with Shinji had overlapped with Nao and his duty to the Matsukawa.

The crack of static pulled Aki's attention back to Kohta. He grumbled about only getting the jazz station and searched for another.

"It would be easier to check the weather if there was a TV here," Kohta said.

"It's not like we have one back home."

"We've got Nao to thank for that." Kohta rolled his eyes. "I mean, I could've been in my hotel with a three-K TV mounted on the wall and no fear I'd be shot in the middle of the night."

"We don't have to worry about that anymore."

"Just the dead bodies and bloodstains on my clothes."

Aki ignored Kohta. It was for the best, since if he encouraged him, Kohta would've ranted about dry cleaning or how hard it was to find the same clothes secondhand. Aki filled the water boiler and set it for oolong tea. Eventually Nao would come down the mountain, and Aki would be ready to serve him a perfect cup of tea.

"Did you find Shinji yet?" Aki asked.

Kohta shrugged. "He wasn't downstairs when the Mafu-fugumi guys got the door open and checked on the ladies."

Aki pressed his lips together. Nao would never lie to him. Still, Aki wanted to see the video posted on the website himself.

Standing before Shinji's room, Aki's skin prickled and the raw tips of his earlobes itched. He grabbed the laptop hidden underneath the bed and sat on the cold floor. The computer felt too heavy in his lap, and his finger hovered over the tracking pad a bit too long. He closed his eyes and blew his hair out of his eyes.

Aki slashed his finger across the trackpad, and the glow of the screen lit the room. He canceled the video upload. Watanabe would have enough on his mind smoothing over his relationship with the Russian mob not to care about a few hours without an upload. He clicked back to the website. The thumbnails gave a clear enough idea of what they were about since the video titles were a string of hot words for searches engines.

After a few minutes clicking around, Aki found himself, or more specifically his engorged member, sticking up in the center of the thumbnail. He clicked on it, and the video played out. A part of himself wanted to piece together the drug-induced fog of pleasure, but he paused it as soon as Shinji said his first "baby."

When Aki scrolled down, the second video of him with Shinji popped up in the "what to watch next" section, but the most disgusting part was the comments. Whatever lewd thing they said, the admin had another that plunged into Aki. Worse were the ones promising a video to come. The time stamp would place the comments after Aki had asked Shinji to delete the video. He'd been used from the moment Shinji had laid eyes on him, and he'd thought of how he could make a profit. Aki slammed the computer shut and covered his face with his hand.

Aki rubbed his eyes with the heels of his palms. He shouldn't have strayed from his devotion to Nao.

Aki's muscles tightened, and his jaw clenched.

Shinji would pay for what he'd done.

Aki grabbed the laptop and stormed out of Shinji's room. The bastard still hadn't shown himself, so he must've been hiding where no one would bother to look.

Aki opened the door the one of the Russians' rooms. Ivan's dead body lay on the bed with a sheet over him. The metal suitcase lay beside him on the foot of the bed. Aki opened it, and all the gold bars were neatly in place.

A faint mumbling then a gasp came from the other side of the room. Aki approached the closet where the noise seemed to come from and slid open the door. Shinji sat hunched in the corner, his body trembling as he covered his head. All those muscles were for show.

He was a shit yakuza.

Aki cleared his throat, and Shinji looked up.

"Oh, it's you, baby," Shinji said.

"Call me baby one more time and I'll shoot your dick off," Aki said between clenched teeth.

"What's gotten into you?"

"You've been hiding in this closet since the Russians attacked."

"They dragged me in here once Ivan died."

"More like you volunteered to go in here since it would be the safest place. The possibility of helping me as I got shot at must've never crossed your mind."

Shinji ran his fingers through his hair. "Babe, really—"

"I said don't call me that."

Aki pulled out the gun from his back waistband and pointed it at Shinji. He held up his hands, the right one shaking.

"Hey, now, why are you pointing that at me?"

"Because I want to make sure you listen to me this time."

Aki shoved the laptop into Shinji's face, but he only looked up at Aki.

"W-what are you talking about?"

"You uploaded the videos without my permission. I want them gone."

Shinji's bottom lip quivered. "B—But—"

Aki put his finger on the trigger. "Now."

The front of Shinji's pants darkened. Aki's eyes narrowed. "Are you pissing yourself?" he asked.

"Shit."

"Fucking coward," Aki hissed. "I said delete the videos."

Shinji looked down for a brief second before grabbing the computer and deleting the videos.

He'd be happy when he could get back home and leave Shinji and the memory of their relationship buried underneath a blizzard of snow.

"There, it's done. J-just don't shoot."

Aki put the gun back into his waistband and refreshed the website. The videos of him were gone. The scent of piss saturated the air, and Aki held his arm over his nose to prevent him from gagging.

"Is it saved anywhere?" Aki asked.

Shinji shook his head. "No, no."

"Good, because if I ever see any of it on the internet, I know exactly who to come looking for."

"Wait, Aki."

"What could you possibly say to me?" Aki shook his head. "Don't even get me started with how disgusting it is that you filmed children. That alone would be justification to shoot you."

"The website was bleeding money. I had to do something, or else Watanabe was going to shut the whole thing down."

"Yori already explained it all. You're a fucking monster. Watanabe didn't put a gun to your head and scream 'film or I'll shoot!'" Aki groaned. "What you did was inhuman."

"Let me explain."

"The only thing you should do right now is change your clothes and make sure I never lay eyes on you again."

Aki slammed the door shut then grabbed the briefcase.

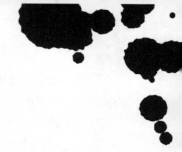

CHAPTER 33

• • •

"**D**O YOU THINK they're overfeeding her?" Nao asked.

Aki leaned closer to get a better view of Nao's phone. Aki had already read all the emails during the train ride back to Sapporo. Everything back home was thankfully quiet, and Nao had promised Kurosawa there'd be hell to pay for trying to keep information away from him. With all that squared away, it left Nao with nothing to do other than to examine the photos of his cat, Nobu, that the new recruits took a few times a day. Aki had gathered them all in a file for him.

"Maybe she looks bigger because she's getting older," Aki said. "Maybe it's because you haven't seen her in a week?"

"I don't want her to get fat."

"It's probably because she doesn't have any fur, so it's hard to tell."

"That must be it." Nao nodded. "The cat I had before Nobu got so chubby."

"Really?"

Nao gave a bitter smile. "I tried a few diets and played with her, but she still looked like a little bear. She'd lay around on my shoes all day."

"Maybe if we keep Nobu lean, she'll grow to be a little panther."

Kohta laughed. "Yeah, a hairless panther."

"Have you ever had a cat?" Nao asked, arcing a brow to Aki.

"No. My family could never afford to keep any pets."

"Really?"

"My grandparents were poor, and when they died, my mother never really brought home food, let alone a pet."

Nao leaned back and closed his eyes. It would be nice to continue the simple conversations over brunch again. Maybe he'd start asking Kohta to watch the restaurant's entry so Aki would have a chance to speak. It was only in the quiet moments that Nao could feel closer to Aki, since they could never step outside a platonic relationship.

"Do you like Nobu?" Nao asked.

"She's a very sweet cat."

"Then we can share her."

The train rolled to a stop, and Nao stood. They got out, and between Aki and Kohta, they carried the luggage off the train.

Nao stepped onto the platform, and Jun emerged from the crowd.

"Father Murata, I'm so glad for your return." Jun's language was formal, and he gave a little bow at the end.

Nao narrowed his eyes. Jun's skin glowed, and his posture was much too relaxed for someone who had just been released from jail. Aki had read all the communication that they had missed while in isolation.

"When were you released?" Nao asked.

Watanabe walked up and slapped Jun on the back. "We got him out the morning after you left, as promised."

"If I'd never gotten arrested, I would've done the little errand with the Russians and you needn't have gone," Jun said, then side-eyed Aki. "I'm surprised he hasn't taken the task on himself."

"You'd be mistaken, then. Running such an expensive errand, I'd want to handle it myself."

Watanabe cleared his throat. "We treated Jun as any allied guest, didn't we?"

Jun patted his stomach. "I think I'll have to hit the gym with all the delicious food we ate."

The veins in Nao's wrist pulsed. He reached out and snatched the end of Jun's tie and jerked him close. Jun's strangled yelp brought pleasure to Nao's ears.

"Just when did you think it would be a good idea to tell me about your release?" Nao hissed.

Jun rasped out something, but Nao's hold was too tight for him to produce words. Jun clawed at his collar, but Nao only pulled tighter.

"Aki." Nao turned to him. "I'm correct. We never received any communication from Jun?"

"None whatsoever," Aki confirmed.

"Were you too busy stuffing your face to call?"

"Fa-Mur..."

Nao groaned, released the tie, and pushed Jun to the ground. Nao stood, arms lax at his side. A few bystanders stopped, but with a glare from Watanabe, they scurried off.

"Explain yourself," Nao ordered.

Jun tugged at his tie and gulped down the air. "I-I did call."

"Are you calling my secretary a liar?"

"No-no. I would never accuse him of that."

"Each word you speak is only making me angrier. I assume you do want to come back on the flight home with us."

"Yes."

"Good, because you know I don't care how high up you are. You are replaceable, and you'll be just another missing person report on the desk of the Kyoto police like everyone else who dares to cross me."

Jun covered his face with a shaky hand and muttered to himself. He bowed his head and squished his legs closer, like if he tried enough, he'd disappear from Nao's sharp gaze.

"I'm waiting for an answer!" Nao yelled.

"I—"

"Boss," Kohta said. "He left a voicemail on my phone."

Nao's eyes narrowed. "And you're just now realizing it?"

"I was checking up on other things since the phone's been without services."

Nao turned his attention back to Jun. "Was my phone not good enough?"

"I must've gotten the number wrong. They took my phone

and wouldn't let me have it back to make a call. I swear I thought it was yours."

Nao's flexed his fist. It sounded like an excuse, but maybe he was trying to save face for Watanabe.

"Get off the floor," Nao said.

Jun stood and brushed the dust off his pants. "I'm sorry about the trouble it has caused."

Nao crossed his arms. "Funny, I'm bad with numbers too. So looks like your paycheck with be zero for the next few months. Aki, make a note to speak to Oshiro and have Jun's pay put into the recreation fund for the rest of the members. Since he spent his time here on vacation."

"I would be more than happy to fulfill your request."

Jun shoved his hands into his pockets, but Nao could see they were forming fists. Next time he'd learn not to fuck up.

"Murata," Watanabe said once it became clear Nao had nothing more to say to Jun. "You must be tired after your trip. I arranged a hotel and made a dinner reservation at a wonderful Greek restaurant."

A curt laugh left Nao. "That would be impossible. We've been away from home long enough. Aki has already arranged our flight back to Kyoto. We leave in three hours."

"I see. It's an off time, so it might take a while to find a restaurant that's open."

"Excuse me for my interruption," Aki said, his voice bringing a smile to Nao's face. "I know a place. They serve a delicious soup curry and would be open."

"Soup curry?" Watanabe's face scrunched.

"That's a Sapporo dish, isn't it?" Nao asked.

"Something more exotic would delight the taste buds more. Don't you think? I know a Greek—"

"I've already made up my mind."

Nao strolled ahead before Watanabe could make another protest.

CHAPTER 34

• • •

THE SMALL FAMILY-OWNED restaurant was everything Nao could have asked for. The main dining area could hold less than twenty but had a private tatami room they gave their yakuza guests. Nao hoped their food was as good as their hospitality, but if the food displayed on the street outside tasted as good as it looked, Nao was in for at least one good thing to come out of his trip.

"This was an excellent suggestion," Nao said.

"It was nothing." Aki smiled. "This restaurant has been part of this family for five generations."

"That's amazing. We should be able to taste their dedication in the soup. Have you eaten here before, Watanabe?"

"I enjoy foreign food more."

"I suspected as much." Nao sighed and traced the clean edge of the low lacquered table. "Really, it's more a disgraceful shame than anything else. One of Japan's highlights is the four seasons and the traditional food coming with each."

Watanabe had kept the scrunched look on his face since they'd left the train station, so the added upturned lip didn't affect Nao. His patience for the Mafufugumi godfather was as short as Kyoto allowed his love life to be. Still, Nao would make the best of the trip he could, even if it was only a quick curry soup and a lingering memory of a kiss he'd grown to regret.

Nao glanced to the metal briefcase between him and Aki holding the gold bars he'd gathered. Beginning to distance himself from Aki was probably the best idea to give Aki a long and healthy life. Aki smiled at him in a knowing way, like he finally understood Nao's reasoning to pluck their relationship off before it could bloom.

A knock came from the other side of the screen door, and Nao welcomed the waitstaff in. They delivered each of their curry soups and accompanying bowl of rice. The room filled with the vibrant smell of black cardamom and fresh ginger.

Nao scooped up a bit of rice and dipped the spoon into his soup to gather the broth. Eaten together, the spices dulled, creating a sweet heat that warmed Nao on the cold winter's day. Silence fell as everyone took their first few bites, but then little moans of pleasure filled the room.

"This is so delicious," Kohta said.

Others echoed the same sentiment.

Each fried mushroom was more savory than the last, and the sweet kabocha slices brought an exciting new sweetness to the dish. Watanabe didn't speak as Nao finished eating the food. Every last drop of Nao's soup found his stomach. Aki had made a little crane out of his chopstick wrapper.

He almost wanted to order another bowl to make up for the disgusting French dishes Watanabe had served him the first night. Nao sighed, but it would be impossible. He could feel the city tugging him back.

He'd been away from home for too long.

Watanabe cleared his throat as Nao put down his spoon on the last bite. "Should we get to formalities?"

"It seems we've reached that time."

Nao finished the last bit of sake in his bowl before placing it before Watanabe for refilling. Once it was filled, Nao mirrored Watanabe, but with his bowl.

"To the union of the Mafufugumi and the Matsukawa," Watanabe said and took his sip of sake.

Nao held up his bowl but did not take a drink. "Yori was a very gracious host considering I overstayed."

"I'll be sure to pass along your thanks." Watanabe's bushy eyebrows drew closer.

"Giichi was especially gracious since I took over his bedroom."

"What are you getting at, Murata?"

Nao lowered his sake bowl and stared Watanabe down before opening the briefcase beside him and Aki. Nao caressed one of the bars and held it.

"There was a fire in your filming studio a few weeks back," Nao said. "It seems like the only person qualified to handle children in that tiny village is Yori."

"How—"

"Maybe my father filled my head with too many old yakuza sayings, but I still believe we are the voice for those who cannot speak. *Children* have no voice and can't make any decisions for themselves. I expect any ally of the Matsukawa to have no business with them." Nao dropped the bar of gold onto the table. The bowls of curry rattled as the brick landed with a thud. "This should help with that decision."

Yori didn't deserve to have the weight of the children's death eat away at her. Even more, Nao didn't want Watanabe to make another quick buck off a similar scheme. Hopefully she'd be able to find all of them before the snow melted.

One of Watanabe's caterpillar eyebrows rose. "Shinji told me what happened between you and the Russians. I have to deal with that fallout."

"Then you'll know how serious I am about people keeping their word. If you drink that sake, I expect you to keep it. Believe me, I'll come up here if I have to, and I really hate leaving my city, so I'll be in a very sour mood. If the Russian leaders ask, tell them they got lost in the blizzard. Shinji knows how to lie."

Watanabe pushed the gold to one of his entourage and smiled. "Of course. The Mafufugumi will honor all our agreements with the Matsukawa."

"Good. Then to the union of our families."

Nao held up his sake bowl and took his sip. Watanabe and Nao exchanged bowls and finished the rest of the sake within. With that, their alliance was sealed.

Nao stood. "Kyoto's waiting for us."

CHAPTER 35

ONE HOUR AND thirty minutes and Nao would be home. His foot tapped on the floor of the private jet, but no matter the luxury, Nao couldn't stop counting down the minutes until his return.

Nao could barely concentrate on what he'd do first once he got home. He'd ask Aki to prepare a pot of oolong tea. While Nao waited for the water to boil, he'd play with his cat. Hopefully she wasn't the kind of cat who snubbed her owner if he was gone for a day. Once the tea was ready, he and Aki would share the pot like they had done every morning. Then Nao would want a full report from Kurosawa about what had happened while he was away and a detailed explanation for why he thought it was within his power to put his secretary in a position to lie for him. Sure, they'd called on the train, but the coded messages they could say over the phones lacked detail.

"Don't we own part of a film studio?" Kohta asked.

"We own a large share of a small film company, yes," Nao said. "It's a safer way to launder money since the anti-yakuza laws placed a stranglehold on the stock market."

"Good. So it would be easy to expand it to a porn label."

Nao crossed his arms. "No. It does yakuza movies and period pieces."

"Well, then we could do period porn or yakuza porn. I'm sure that's a fetish for someone out there."

Aki rolled his eyes. "You're in one and you suddenly think you can be a porn star."

"How else am I supposed to get girls?" Kohta clasped his hands together. "Boss, please. You have me working twenty-four seven."

"You just had a vacation."

"That wasn't a vacation. Jun was the only one who got to enjoy himself during the whole trip. I was too worried about getting stabbed in the back to have a good time."

Aki laughed. "You sure played enough poker to look like you were on vacation."

One hour and twenty-three minutes.

"Please, Boss, even Aki's tired of hearing me talk, and I'm sure he'd love it if I was gone at least one day out of the week."

"I'll look for another bodyguard so you two could trade off days," Nao said.

Aki mouthed *ungrateful bastard* at Kohta, but the blond seemed unfazed.

Nao smiled. "Should I get an extra secretary, so you could get a few days off a week, too?"

"It's my pleasure to serve you daily, Father Murata."

Kohta rolled his eyes and mouthed *workaholic.*

Maybe a private jet wasn't the best way to go. Kohta took it as an opportunity to fill up the time with random chatter. It meant not having to check in through an airport, so that was faster. The four bars of gold they carried wouldn't do well going through a commercial flight's security.

Kohta stretched out his arms. "When we get home, the first thing I want to do is take a nap. Traveling always makes me tired."

"Why don't you try taking one now?" Nao suggested.

Aki and Jun laughed, but Aki's phone ringing cut it short.

"This is Hisona," Aki answered.

Nao was too far away to distinguish the voice coming from the other phone, but the way Aki rubbed his hand on his pant leg didn't look good.

"Without fail." Aki held out the phone to Nao. "The Korean mob attacked one of the safehouses. It's war."

Nao grabbed the phone. "Kurosawa?"

"What's our next move, Father Murata?" he asked.

Nao licked his lips. In a little over an hour, they'd taste his blade yet again. He could slaughter one hundred more to bring peace back to the city.

"It's time to annihilate them once and for all."

◆ ◆ ◆

Look for

FLOWERS OF FLESH AND BLOOD

the next book in the

THE YAKUZA PATH

series, coming soon.

Check out Amy's YouTube for behind-the-scenes updates.

WWW.YOUTUBE.COM/USER/AMYTASUKADA

A NOTE
• • •

DEAR READER,

Thank you so much for your patience with waiting for *The Deafening Silence* to come out. I admit it took me longer than I wanted. I herniated two discs in my spine at the start of writing it and the twice-weekly visits to physical therapy exhausted me so much I ended up needing to push the date back. Thank you to everyone who sent me well wishes. They were a big help on the days I wanted to sleep away in bed but knew I had to get up and at least write something.

I admit when I was writing the scene where Nao and Aki kissed, I had planned it to be a simple peck on the cheek, but when it came down to writing it, they got a whole make-out session! I've been wanting those two to have a real kiss for the longest time, and all of sudden they were. Of course, I couldn't take it out once it was down on paper. Hopefully it hasn't disappointed too many of you. I promise the push and pull of Nao's and Aki's relationship will have a resolution in the next book.

Speaking of the next book, I am not sure when it will come out. I hate to leave it open like that, but it's important to me that it's good and that I don't want to say one date and have to change it. The best thing would be to subscribe to my YouTube channel. I usually give a weekly update on Monday with what I've been working on. Just know that while a few other yakuza romances feed the beast that is the Amazon algorithm.

Until then, if you could leave a review of this book, it would help me out tremendously. Tell your friends about the series; that way you can talk about it with someone else. I promise more kissing in the next book…but I won't say from who.

Thanks again!

Amy Tasukada

October 2018

ABOUT THE AUTHOR

• • •

AMY TASUKADA LIVES lives in North Texas with a calico cat called O'Hara. As an only child her day dreams kept her entertained, and at age ten she started to put them to paper. Since then her love of writing hasn't cease. She can be found drinking hot tea and filming Japanese street fashion hauls on her Youtube channel.

CONNECT WITH AMY ON...
Website: AmyTasukada.com
Facebook: Facebook.com/amytasukadaofficial
Twitter: Twitter.com/amytasukada
Youtube: YouTube.com/user/amytasukada

CPSIA information can be obtained
at www.ICGtesting.com
Printed in the USA
BVHW081001130820
586318BV00002B/412